KINFOLK

MATT KURTZ

GRINDHOUSE
PRESS

Grindhouse Press
PO BOX 521
Dayton, Ohio 45401

Grindhouse Press #043
ISBN-10: 1-941918-37-9
ISBN-13: 978-1-941918-37-1

Other titles by Matt Kurtz

Monkey's Box of Horrors - Tales of Terror: Volume 1
Monkey's Bucket of Horrors - Tales of Terror: Volume 2

ONE

IT HAD BEEN A LONG day for twenty-year-old Andy Meyerson. One that had gone horribly wrong in the blink of an eye. Exhausted, parched, and hungry, he shambled along the deserted farm road as the sun began its descent. The approaching darkness served as a grim reminder he'd made many poor decisions along his short journey, choices that were inevitably going to cost him his life.

Andy's original intention was simple ...

For one month, he planned to travel from coast to coast to see America. It was a family tradition, a rite of passage, that both of his older brothers had partaken and one their father had invented some thirty years ago. The rules were simple: drive the designated course to see the top landmarks and cities of the continental forty-eight, rough it by sleeping under the stars, and enjoy the dusk of youth before adulthood threw its responsibilities your way upon college graduation. Using the buddy system for safety and companionship, along with whomever had the most reliable vehicle, a Meyerson boy and select friend journeyed the same route first established by Dad before his own graduation. So instead of heading home for summer break, Andy invited his dormmate Frank to accompany him on this journey of a lifetime. With his girlfriend Jessica's blessing, Frank not only agreed to the trip but volunteered the use of his new Cadillac Escalade, a gift from his parents for not failing any classes two consecutive semesters. In the Caddy, they'd travel in style and always have a comfortable place to sleep in at designated rest stops along the way.

All was smooth for the first few days until Frank's crippling insecurities cut their trip short after Jessica became harder and harder to reach. Andy tried to convince him things were fine but Frank felt she only wanted him gone in order to sleep around—reason enough for him to call it quits on Andy and rush back to try to salvage the relationship.

Mistake number one was ever asking Frank to join him. Number two was continuing on without him. But Andy was graduating next spring and knew it was now or never. Avoiding any news of Frank's abandonment to his parents, Andy forged ahead and made his own route, hitching rides wherever they'd take him and bunking in a sleeping bag whenever he found a little shelter. His new plan was to just experience as many of the forty-eight states as possible before his month was up then buy a bus ticket home. Sure, hitchhiking was dangerous, but as long as he followed his gut about the people offering rides, didn't lose his cell phone or his parents' emergency credit card, and always kept his folding Buck knife within reach, Andy figured he'd do just fine.

So began The Meyerson Tour of America 2.0, where the trip was all about the journey, not the destinations.

It was earlier that morning when his real troubles began, after asking for a lift at Crofty's Truck Stop and Diner Grill just outside of Brownsville, Texas. The couple that gave him a ride up to that point dropped him off at the greasy spoon and wished him luck on his adventure. They were nice people in their late fifties, both professors at The University of Texas at Brownsville that Andy met while gambling in Shreveport, Louisiana. His original plan to cross Texas was by way of the Dallas/Fort Worth metroplex before moving west to New Mexico, but hearing how the couple were heading south along the coast, he couldn't resist charting a new course. 'Stay fluid' was his motto nowadays—had to be when depending on the kindness of strangers for your next ride. By accepting their offer, he'd pass through Houston and Corpus Christi on the way to their hometown of Brownsville. From there, he could make a straight shot north to visit San Antonio, Austin, and, finally, Dallas and Fort Worth. He'd be hitting all the major cities of the Lone Star state, something his brothers and Dad never accomplished as their designated course only took them through Dallas/Fort Worth.

With dawn spilling through the truck stop's windows, Andy sat at the end of the Formica bar with a steaming cup of coffee and eyed what might be his northbound prospects.

All two of them.

The first was a fat, bald, middle-aged man reading his bible while slurping his breakfast—a steaming bowl of yesterday's chili. Both looked kind of greasy to Andy.

Option B was a skinny, leathery man with dead, unblinking eyes floating in dark, puffy sockets. He sat in a daze, chainsmoking unfiltered Pall Malls and downing cups of coffee. It was quite obvious the guy was running on fumes, nicotine and caffeine his main subsistence.

So ...

Chainsmoking zombie? Or bible thumper?

Andy exhaled. Slim pickins indeed.

He figured it would probably be easier to zone out during any potential sermons than hack up a lung from all that secondhand smoke. Plus, in choosing Option B, he'd reek of cigarettes, which might offend the next driver he'd meet and cost him a ride.

Feeling it'd be rude to interrupt the fat guy's biblical breakfast in order to confirm which way he was heading, Andy waited until the man finished his meal then followed him out into the lot. As the trucker walked around his tractor-trailer and did a quick, pre-trip inspection, Andy pulled out a black Sharpie and pushed up the sleeve on his left arm. The underside of his forearm was covered in faded numbers and letters. License plates numbers. Confident he'd get a ride with the man, he drew a line through the darkest six-digit set belonging to that nice Brownsville couple and wrote down the tractor's plates. Andy figured if a ride became trouble, he'd have something to ID them with to the authorities. Writing it on his arm was a guaranteed way to always keep the info on him, unlike a note-pad that could easily be lost or stolen. He quickly pulled down his sleeve to cover the latest entry then moved in.

"Excuse me, sir," he said.

Caught off guard, the man gasped and spun around. He eyed Andy up and down, determining if he was a threat ... or worse, selling something.

Andy retreated a few steps, "Sorry about that."

James F. Cooper stared deep into the young man's eyes and flashed a crooked smile. His overly anxious grin and piggy eyes suddenly made Andy's gut squirm. Without thinking, Andy glanced back at the diner where Option B still sat juicing on caffeine and nicotine.

Ya know, maybe choking on some secondhand smoke wouldn't be so bad after all.

"Yes?" James said. "How can I help you, son?"

Andy returned his attention to the man. Or, more specifically, to the bible clutched in his thick fingers.

Okay, the dude's religious. Thou shalt not kill, right? So, I should be okay then. Yeah, right ... ever hear of the crusades, dummy?

He cleared his throat and threw it out there anyway, "Well, if you're heading north and looking for some company, I'd be much obliged for a ride, sir."

The man thought it over for a moment, then nodded, his plump cheeks jiggling long after his head went still. "I'd like that. The company could do me some good. Hop on in."

The ride was smooth until after Andy leaned back in his seat to grab some shut eye. Up until then, much to his surprise, there was very little discussion of religious matters. James had told him he was a happily married man of twenty years with a daughter around Andy's age and a son about to enter junior high. When not on the road, he played the organ at church on Sundays and taught Sunday School—ironically on Tuesday nights—to the junior high age set. Andy hoped to avoid having to reciprocate his own religious history since it could be summed up in a single word—none. So before James had a chance to prod, Andy yawned and said he could sure use some sleep if that was all right. Dropping his bag to the passenger floorboard for a footrest (and to keep it out of reach from any sticky fingers), he leaned back and lowered the brim on his ball cap just enough to still keep tabs on James. Not realizing how exhausted he truly was, Andy closed his eyes and was fast asleep within minutes.

An hour or so later, the loud hiss of air brakes snapped Andy from his deep slumber. James was turned in his direction, staring at him. Smiling.

Andy wiped the sleep from his eyes and glanced out the windshield. They were parked, with engine idling, on a desolate farm road lined with trees.

"What's going on?"

James shrugged. He was trembling, looking more than a little nervous. "You tell me."

"What are we doing here? Why aren't we on the highway?"

"I thought we could be alone. Isn't that why you wanted the ride?" He slowly reached over with a shaky hand for Andy's thigh. "For companionship?"

Andy sat frozen and watched the hovering hand as if it was a cobra poised to strike. It wasn't until James's sweaty palm made contact with his flesh that Andy pushed the hand away. "Jesus, dude! No offense, but I think you got the wrong idea."

James's smile twisted into a sneer. "Please. Don't blaspheme."

"Fine. Whatever. But I'm not gay. I mean, that's fine if you are and all, but please … just … don't touch me. Okay?"

The fat man's lip curled up even further. "I am not a queer, son," James said. His voice grew louder, more intense with each word. "And I'm offended you would accuse me of such grotesque hedonism. For I am a God-fearing man."

"Grotesque hedonism … ?" Andy paused, trying to take it all in. He wanted to say *The only grotesque thing here is your goddamn hypocrisy, you ignorant fuck!* but thought better of it. Best not to let the situation escalate. He waited a few seconds before responding, "You're right, James. You're a good man. But maybe it's best we part ways at the next stop."

The man glared at him in silence.

"James?"

"No. You will exit this cab. Now."

"What?"

"I will not spend another second with someone who has taken advantage of my hospitality and accused me of … of … faggotry."

Andy almost laughed at the man's ignorance until he took another quick glance out the window and saw zero signs of civilization. "Look, James. I'm sorry if I offended you. How 'bout I just sit here with my mouth shut and once you get us back to the highway, you can drop me off on the side of the road."

James's left arm suddenly swung up and over his fat belly before pressing the muzzle of a thirty-eight revolver against Andy's forehead. It's cold steel froze him. Andy remembered the buck knife in the side pocket of his cargo shorts, but it never felt so far away.

"You … will exit this cab. Now."

Andy agreed, but refused to nod. "Okay," he said, barely above a whisper. "Okay. Let me just grab my ..." Andy slowly reached for both the door handle and the bag at his feet.

"Get out now!" James said, thumbing back the hammer. The gun shook in his grasp, either from anger or adrenaline. Whichever the reason, it scared the holy hell out of Andy. An unintentional twitch of the trigger finger could send his brain exploding through the passenger window. It was best to forget about his bag for the moment and carefully slide out of the cab to a safer distance. Once on the ground, he'd ask James for his belongings.

Andy slowly opened the door and raised both hands in the air. His heart hammered in his chest even harder when he was forced to put his back to James in order to climb out. Once turned, Andy whimpered as the cold muzzle pressed against the base of his skull.

"Move!" James commanded.

Andy dropped to the ground and, before he could slowly turn to ask for his bag, the shrieking hiss of the air brakes almost made him leap out of his skin. The engine revved and the tractor gunned ahead, the momentum slamming the passenger door closed and slinging the attached trailer forward with a loud crack. As the truck picked up speed along the gravel road, Andy stood planted, completely dumbstruck over what just took place.

"But ... but, my bag ..."

The semi disappeared around a tree-lined curve and the roar of its engine gradually faded. It took a moment for Andy to snap out of his daze. He looked around and instinctively reached into his pocket for his cell phone but it wasn't there. He patted both sides of his cargo shorts then paused and groaned.

His phone was still charging in the tractor's cab.

"Shit!"

Andy inhaled sharply and checked his surroundings. It appeared to be the middle of nowhere. But the highway couldn't be too far away, right? He lowered his head and listened for the distant sound of traffic to guide his way. He heard nothing except for a few birds chirping, a gentle breeze swaying the treetops, and his own racing heart still pounding in his ears.

Okay. Don't panic, he told himself. *It's only*, he checked his watch, *nine-forty in the morning.* That gave him plenty of time to reach some place with a phone before nightfall. He took a deep breath then started down the road in the direction the tractor-trailer disappeared, hoping a gas station lay just beyond the bend.

Nearly eleven hours later, with the sun starting to set, Andy fought to stay focused. He'd chosen the wrong path at the fork in the road too many miles back. The dirt road ahead had narrowed to a single lane that seemed to lead deeper into the sticks.

Sunburned and possibly running a fever from oncoming dehydration, Andy shivered and collapsed on a rotten log beside the road. The sun dipped below the treetops and a wave of shadows moved across him. He pulled up his collar as a chill slithered up his spine. It was going to be a long night, one barely illuminated by the crescent moon already visible in the purple sky. Best to set up camp now. Clear the brush of any spiders, snakes, and fire-ant mounds that might sting or bite under the cover of darkness.

He slowly inhaled, still unable to fathom how things had sped so quickly out of control. It went without saying that his little adventure was officially over. Once he reached a phone, he'd tell his parents the truth then figure out the fastest way home.

Taking in the utter isolation, a rising panic worked its way up from the pit of his belly. Andy quickly swallowed it back down and tried to remain optimistic. Things could always be worse, right?

As if on cue, a coyote howled somewhere in the distance. It's call slowly faded into a low rumble.

Andy spun. Squinting in the gloom, he saw the approaching vehicle in what remained of the sun's final light. An old, orange pickup with an oversized, white camper attached to its bed moved in his direction at a slow and steady pace.

Springing to his feet, Andy stepped into the dirt road and waved at the truck. Its headlights flashed twice in acknowledgment. The vehicle crept up to him then stopped, its brakes letting off an ear-piercing squeal.

Andy glanced down at the truck's license plate and quickly repeated the numbers and letters to commit them to memory—or at least until he could secretly write them down once settled in for the ride.

Walking to the driver's side window, he smiled and hoped his luck had finally changed for the better.

"Wake up."

A grimy, callused hand slapped his face.

Andy gave a snorting intake of breath. His eyes snapped open and fought to focus. When they finally did, his assailant had already slunk back into the shadows.

Gagged with an oily rag, Andy lay on his belly with a pillow shoved under his hips. He let out a muffled cry and tried to spring to his feet but the rope binding his wrist and ankles to the bed frame kept him prone, spread eagle—face down, ass up—on the blood and shit-stained mattress.

The room was murky. The air thick.

It smelled like the den of a wild animal.

Above the bed, a one hundred-watt bulb, housed in a cheap metal reflector dome, hung low from the ceiling by way of extension cord. Beyond its beam, the room fell to an inky abyss.

Remembering the knife in his shorts, Andy fought to break free from his restraints to reach it. The bed frame squeaked and the mattress groaned under his jerky movement.

In the darkness, someone cleared their throat.

Andy froze. Only his bloodshot eyes shifted in their glistening sockets, attempting to locate the person.

While he searched, his fevered brain raced to recall how he got there ... Waving down the orange pickup for a ride. The passenger seat full of stinking burlap bags. The old man behind the wheel, thumbing over his shoulder to the white, oversized camper. The man telling him to hop in back. The tailgate opening, an invitation extended. Going to the rear. Gazing into the camper. Scalp prickling at the sight of the two—

A small light clicked on in the corner. The sound made Andy jump and snapped him back to the present.

Across the room, a man stood at an old triple dresser. His back was to Andy. The reflection in the mirror mounted to the piece of furniture was blocked by the man's body. He adjusted the small desk lamp atop the dresser then carefully arranged the items along its surface with a metallic clanking sound.

Biting his gag, Andy squinted to get a better look at his captor.

The man was tall, lanky, and dressed in dirty, rumpled clothes. Although crowned bald, his long locks in back cascaded to his shoulders in a greasy mullet. He shifted slightly and his face came into view in the mirror. Andy narrowed his eyes for a better look then realized the man was already glaring back at him in the reflection. The man wiggled his thick brows and grinned.

Andy gasped and looked away. Any possibility of release might depend on how little he saw of his captor. If the man felt Andy could identify him, the chances of him getting out alive would probably be next to none. Unfortunately, a quick glimpse was all it took to sear his image on Andy's brain. The long, hooked nose. Round, thick, coke-bottle glasses. And those greasy, bushy, pork chop sideburns that resembled a nest of daddy longleg spiders resting on each cheek.

Still studying Andy in the mirror, the man with pork chop sideburns licked his flaking lips then went back to the items on the dresser.

Filled with dread, Andy forced himself to look back at Pork

Chop to see what he was doing. His eyes widened in terror when the man held a straight razor to the lamp, the light glinting off its polished blade.

Pork Chop plucked a thumb over the sharpened edge. "Yeahhhhh …" he said, whispering. "Is good."

A whimper escaped Andy.

"Shuddup," Pork Chop said without missing a beat.

Terrified, Andy went silent.

Pork Chop slowly turned and approached the bed, a sardonic grin accompanying the straight razor in his hand. "But don't worry. You can make all the noise ya want in just a bit."

With those words, any hope of a safe release vanished. Andy writhed and tried again for the knife in his pocket but the ropes binding him offered no slack.

Pork Chop jumped on the bed and quickly mounted his captive's back. Andy tried to buck him off, but Pork Chop hooked both legs under him and dug in deep. He grabbed Andy by the scruff of his collar and slapped his ass like riding an ornery bull. "That's right! Fight! Fight, boy!"

And Andy fought like hell as the razor sliced his clothes up the back. Within seconds, he was stripped to only his briefs.

"What's this?" Pork Chop jabbed a finger at the writing in marker that covered Andy's forearm. "Them some sort of tattoo?" He wrenched Andy's arm up for a closer look—at least as far as the restraints allowed. Andy squealed in equal parts fear and pain.

"Asked you what it is? Now tell me!"

Andy tried to comply behind the gag, but of course it was unintelligible.

A loud crash came from outside the room.

Pork Chop released Andy's arm and whirled around to the closed bedroom door. Shadows moved within the bright light at its threshold.

Inaudible shouting. More crashes and heavy thuds. The commotion was moving closer.

Returning to Andy, Pork Chop leaned in and gave him a gentle pat. "'Kay, looks like playtime's over. Hold still, now." Using the full weight of his body to inflict maximum damage, he slammed his elbow into the base of Andy's skull. The impact of bone against bone made a sickening crack.

Andy's head snapped forward then back and his body arched. Pork Chop unleashed another vicious elbow strike to the back of the head. Then another. Andy went limp, collapsing to the mattress where he floated in and out of consciousness. A gurgle escaped his throat then he stared blankly into the abyss before him.

Pork Chop leaned forward and pressed his lips to Andy's ear. "Sorry 'bout that, hoss. Just had to sedate ya a bit. You'll thank me later." Noticing the blood trickling down Andy's nape, Pork Chop licked at it sensually, savoring its coppery taste. His tongue traced the young man's skull and worked its way up through his blood-drenched hair. When it slid off Andy's scalp, Pork Chop shuddered and flicked his tongue in an obscene display of mock cunninglingus.

"Mmmm-mmm! Fear tastes good on ya, boy. Precious is gonna love him some of that."

The bedroom door burst open. The hall light flooded into the room and across the bed. Andy slid his glazed eyes in the direction of the behemoth shambling closer through the open doorway. The wood floor creaked under its massive weight.

Before Pork Chop could move out of the way, a gigantic hand hooked around his neck and violently wrenched him off the bed. The scrawny man crashed to the hardwood floor and yelped in pain. "I's just tenderizin' the meat! Don't be such a goddamn—!"

A snarl cut him off.

Pork Chop retreated, scuttling to the safety of the dark corner. "Yep, you got it. He's all yours! All yours!"

The giant stood beside the bed and stared down at Andy.

Silence. Then a groan of approval.

The hulking mass climbed on top of Andy, crushing him into the mattress. Andy tried to turn to his assailant and beg for mercy but a filthy hand with long cracked nails slammed his head back down into the pillow.

His briefs were ripped from his hips and tossed aside.

Andy cried out when he heard the undoing of a zipper behind him. After a hearty hack, a warm glob of spit landed between his ass-cheeks and slid deeper into his crack. With his face smashed into the bed, Andy croaked a final, muffled plea that went unheard.

Pork Chop rocked with excitement in the dark corner, ready to enjoy the show that was about to get real messy.

Andy squealed upon penetration. He thrust his hips into the soiled mattress in a futile attempt to escape the burning agony plowing into him. The giant's body enveloped the young man's entire backside as he lay on top, pumping away, grunting like a wild animal. Slick belly fat slapped against the small of Andy's back, causing a disgusting suction noise. The hot air in the room now reeked of body odor and feces.

Unable to fight, Andy squeezed his eyes shut and tried to leave his body. *I wanna go home. Please let me go home.*

Then, from over his shoulder, a large, gaping mouth lunged forward and bit into his neck, tearing away a meaty chunk of his upper trapezius in a shower of blood and stretching sinew.

Andy howled in agony behind his gag while being eaten alive. Loud, feral chewing invaded his ears as the violent pounding at his ass increased in its intensity from the bloodlust. A second bite removed a piece of his shoulder.

The horizon suddenly shifted. He was going into shock. His eyes rolled back in his head and his body went limp.

The giant reached around and slid his hand under Andy's chin, lifting his head, folding him back until the base of his skull was pinned against his shoulder blades. Then, like scraping the flesh off an artichoke petal, the large mouth with jagged teeth clamped over

MATT KURTZ

Andy's hairline and raked back, tearing loose part of his scalp. The hairy, crimson ribbons stretched and snapped like taut rubber bands, exposing Andy's skull. Blood flowed ... soaking mattress, man, and beast. The scalp flap was spit aside. The hungry mouth went for the bubbling head wound and slurped at the crimson fluid with child-like glee.

Like a dog waiting for scraps, Pork Chop watched from the shadows and listened to the chewing, sucking, and squeaking of bedsprings—the beautiful cacophony of pleasure and slaughter filling his ears. He hoped this time Precious wouldn't be so greedy and would save some of the good parts for both he and the rest of the family ... as the rumbling in his belly signaled dinnertime was almost here.

TWO

THE LAST CHANCE **BAR, AN** alcoholic purgatory for souls preferring to stay lost, sat isolated along the South Texas country road. Sulfur lamps cast their sickly, jaundiced glow over the parking lot and battled the veil of darkness wanting to consume the roadside watering hole. The glitter of broken glass on asphalt reflected both streetlamp and full moon above as a legion of crickets hopped across the various makes and models of clunkers scattered throughout the lot.

The growl of an engine sounded somewhere in the distance then headlights pierced the horizon. Like an approaching storm, the lights got brighter and the engine's rumble grew louder until a polished black 1967 Ford Galaxie materialized out of the shadows. The vehicle slowed to a stop in the middle of the street in front of the bar with its muffler chugging, dripping exhaust. The splattered remains of moths, lacewings, and other insects continued baking on its grill and headlamps.

The engine revved, the Galaxie slowly turning and gliding into the parking lot like a great white shark seeking prey.

With his head hung low, Ray Kuttner sat alone in the back of the murky bar. His humble surroundings were decorated with faded beer posters permanently stained yellow from decades of nicotine-laced smoke. To his left, a dilapidated pool table was shoved against the wall, its felt top torn and buried under an avalanche of empty liquor boxes.

Across the way, an ancient bartender held a trembling mug to a tap as its pipes farted out more air than actual beer. Once the glass was three quarters full—any more would only slosh over the sides in his tremored grasp—he placed it in front of the hunched drunk parked on the opposite side then shuffled away without a word.

About a half dozen patrons peppered the place, all nearly twice the age of Ray's thirty-five years. They sat isolated, silent, lost in thought or listening to a country crooner crackling from the blown-out speaker on a half-lit jukebox.

This wasn't a place for social gathering or celebration. It was for the lost and weary seeking liquid refuge from their shitty existence.

At the back table, Ray fidgeted with what hung from the silver necklace stretched from his open collar. He eyed the large whiskey tumbler in his other hand and licked his lips in anticipation of its contents. His truck keys were pushed aside, resting next to a dirty ashtray and an unlit candle housed in a gaudy glass globe. A line of shots covered the table and a number of empties had yet to be gathered by a wait staff consisting of a lone, blue-haired elderly woman wearing more garish face paint than a rodeo clown. Sitting behind the bar, she was far too busy smacking gum and painting her talons with nail polish to give two shits about her cheapskate customers and their lack of tips. If they wanted another cold one, they could get off their pruned asses and come to her.

The front door opened, sucking out a cloud of smoke that rolled out of the bar and up into the night. The bright yellow lights from the parking lot pierced the hazy atmosphere, eliciting a collective groan that rippled throughout the joint as the wrinkled patrons shielded their eyes or looked away.

Thankfully, the solid metal door quickly slammed shut and sealed the living dead back in their neon-lit tomb.

Ray reached for the next shot in line when a shadow fell over him.

"This seat taken?"

Ray exhaled and quickly tucked the necklace back into his shirt. His bloodshot eyes slid up and glared at the visitor, hoping the look would be a sufficient answer. But the fellow wearing jeans, a button down, and a black leather jacket stood waiting, his face practically swallowed by the shadows. Ray squinted in the dim light to get a better look at the guy's mug to see if the joker was itching to start trouble. Once his eyes adjusted, his jaw fell slack. He scoffed and slowly rose, standing face to face with the man.

"Eric?"

Eric stepped into the light. His face was all smiles. Since a simple handshake wouldn't suffice, he grabbed Ray and hugged him, capping it off with three hearty pats on the back. "Goddamn," Eric said, "you're a hard man to find."

Ray slowly raised his arms and half-heartily returned the gesture. When the room started to tilt, he planted a hand on the table for balance. "Wha …" he said, shaking his head. "What the fuck ya doing here, man?"

Eric caught a hint of annoyance in the man's inflection. "Yeah, good to see you, too."

Ray motioned for Eric to sit. Once they pulled their chairs to the table, Ray slammed a shot. He gave Eric the once over and seemed at a loss for words. His finger frantically tapped the table as if sending a Morse code for help on what to say next.

Eric obliged. "So you weren't kidding when you said you lived in South Texas. Any closer and we'd be stopped by border patrol."

"Guess you've never been down this far, huh?"

"Nope. Never got an invite to. In fact, felt more like you were dodging me."

Eric waited for some sort of response or rebuttal, but received neither. Both looked away and let the silence settle for a bit.

"Well, now that you're here," Ray said, motioning to the bar, "go grab yourself a drink."

Eric almost laughed. There was enough alcohol on the table for a frat party during rush week, but, apparently, it was spoken for. All of it. "Nah, I'm driving tonight."

Ray perked up a little. "Not stickin' around?"

"No. I ... ah ... I kinda have a prior commitment."

"So you drove all this way out here for ... what?"

"For my brother's birthday. Missed the last three. Figured it was more than overdue. I mean, that's what you're celebrating here in this fine establishment, isn't it? Your birthday?"

Knowing it was pathetic, Ray simply shrugged.

"Well, I didn't want you to spend it alone and all. There's no reason for it."

Ray glared at him. "Don't really have a choice nowadays, wouldn't ya say?"

The room dropped a few degrees. Eric sunk in his chair. "I meant ..." He opened his mouth to continue, paused, then looked away to avoid further provoking an angry dog. "Never mind."

Ray backed down slightly. "It's okay."

"Guess that's my cue to address the pink elephant in the room, huh?"

Ray threw back a shot. He needed medication for what was coming.

"For what it's worth ... I'm sorry."

Ray held up a hand. "Please. Just. Don't." He slammed another shot to drown the harsh words wanting to rise.

Eric sat silent and studied Ray. Had it really only been three years since they'd last seen each other? From the deep lines and puffy features plaguing his older brother's face, it seemed more like a decade had passed. The man looked hard. Very hard. And the change wasn't confined to his face either. His familiar plaid shirt once filled by muscular arms and a broad chest now hung loose over his lean frame. Of course, if the amount of empty glasses covering the table were any indication of how he spent his nights— birthday or otherwise—it was no wonder Ray looked so goddamn awful. Like a man who had thrown in the towel long ago and was only abusing what little remained of his life in order to burn it out quicker.

If so, all that was about to change by this one simple visit. It was time to redirect that fire down another path.

Eric cleared his throat. "Like I said, I'm just here for your birthday. Wanna give you a gift. And talk about some things."

"So talk."

Eric waited, took a deep breath, and leaned closer to keep their conversation private. "He was telling the truth. He knew nothing about it."

Ray stared at his whiskey shot. Fidgeted with it. Then slammed it. Afterward, he feigned puzzlement.

"Jacobs," Eric answered. "He wasn't involved."

Ray shook his head and looked away. "Don't know what you're talking about." He moved for another shot but Eric slammed his hand on top of Ray's and pinned it to the table.

"Listen to me, goddammit!" Eric said. "I did a lot of asking around and Jacobs was wasted the night it happened to Rachel."

Ray winced at her name.

Good. Now that Eric knew he had his brother's attention, he released his hand. "I found a guy that was wasted with him on a half g of smack that night. Jacobs was too fucked up to do anything but probably lay around and piss himself."

"And you believe the word of some junkie?"

"Yeah, because he gave me quite an earful. About a score from the previous night that Jacobs was bragging about. The guy told me shit only you, me, and Jacobs would know about it. The timelines match up. I'm tellin' ya, it wasn't him."

"Bullshit!"

"He was scum, Ray. A junkie. A real piece of shit. And I never should've brought him on as our third guy. That was my mistake, something I gotta live with. Everyday. But we killed the wrong guy."

"No. He confessed." Ray kicked back a shot and grabbed another, his fingers tapping rapidly against it.

"Shit, man. The stuff we did to him, I'm surprised he didn't confess to being Jack the fuckin' Ripper. Whatever the case, I promise you he did not kill your wife."

Eric reached into his jacket pocket and removed a sealed business envelope. He gently placed it on top of the shot glasses and smiled.

Ray stared at the envelope, refusing to touch it. He looked at his brother for the answer.

After a long beat, Eric finally gave him that answer. "The name and address of the guy who *did* murder your wife. Happy birthday, Ray."

THREE

ERIC SAW A SPARK OF rage in his brother's eyes and felt certain it wasn't *completely* directed at him for drudging up the past.

At least not yet. He had to be careful and add just the right amount of fuel to put a little heat under Ray's ass. Eric nodded to the envelope. "Oklahoma City. Little over ten hours away. He'll be there just shy of three days to make a drop. Inside is all the needed info. Time. Date. Directions. We leave now. Get there early. Prepare. Wait. Then we nab him and make that motherfucker scream."

Ray narrowed his eyes at his brother.

"This guy is definitely a professional," Eric continued. "Slippery. Always on the move. Only uses a messenger service that keeps him in the shadows. Practically a ghost."

"If he's so hard to pin down, how do *you* know he's making a drop? And where it'll be?"

Eric smiled. "'Cause I set it up. Called in every favor owed and it still wasn't enough. Let's just say that now I owe people. Which makes this a onetime deal." Eric leaned in. "It's now or never, Ray."

Ray stared at the envelope, still refusing to touch it. His hand fidgeted with an empty shot glass then inched closer to his birthday gift. It was like an animal sniffing the air, checking its surroundings one last time before stepping into a trap to take the bait.

Eric watched. Waited.

Then Ray pulled away, leaned back in his chair, and shook his head.

Eric wanted to scream. Was this really that hard of a sell? He expected his brother to already be out the door with directions in hand, leading the way to go dish out some major payback. But apparently the Ray he was hoping to find—the one he *needed* to find—had deflated into this sad shell sitting across from him.

Ray's bloodshot eyes slid up and glared at his younger brother. "Sorry to disappoint ya," he said, reaching for a shot. "But I ain't that man anymore." He slammed the remaining two shots consecutively and exhaled sharply from the burn.

"Damn straight," Eric said. "The guy I knew was a leader. A bad ass. Someone that commanded respect. Not this …" he waved a hand at Ray, "this … pathetic drunk."

"Goodbye, Eric." Ray stood. Eric bolted up and grabbed his arm.

"Okay. Okay. Okay. I'm sorry. Just hold up a sec." Ray shrugged free and Eric held up both hands in mock surrender. "Said I'm sorry. Let's just chill. How about some more drinks? Huh? C'mon, I'm buying. You sit. The next round's on me."

"Good seeing ya. But it's getting late." He pushed past Eric and moved to the bar to pay his tab.

Defeated, Eric went to retrieve the envelope from the table then noticed the truck keys left behind. "Hey! You forgot your ke—" He paused and glanced back at the keys. A smile crept upon his face. He snatched both envelope and keys and shoved them deep into his pocket.

"Forty-three fifty-two," the ancient bartender told Ray.

Ray was surprised over the amount. Then again, he'd lost track of how much booze he ordered. He fished out his wallet and removed all the bills. Squinting in the dim light, he counted the crumpled money. "Five. Ten. Twenty. Twenty-one. Twenty-two." He paused for a moment, either too drunk to keep count or embarrassed he'd come up short. He cleared his throat and started over.

Eric bellied up to the bar beside his brother. Without his keys, Ray would need a ride home. And that would allow Eric a second attempt to win him over. He *might* be able to convince Ray to do what needed to be done but, overall, the odds were not in Eric's favor. What if Ray refused the lift? Or, if he did accept, simply passed out on the ride home? For Eric, that was too much shit stacked against him. Next to cold-cocking the dumb son-of-a-bitch and dragging him into the Galaxie so they could head for the Texas-Oklahoma border, Eric needed to come up with a little something extra to help move things along. A real enema to flush out the shit Ray was bound to pull. Something that would get—and keep—Ray in the car by his own volition.

The bartender patiently stood and waited for Ray to recount his crumpled currency. The register drawer was wide open. Full of cash. Eric shook his head. The old dude was far too trusting—and downright stupid—to leave his till exposed for that long.

Then inspiration struck.

A plan quickly forming, Eric glanced back and forth between his brother and the old man at the register. He'd have to be extremely careful. Take it over the top. In fact, go completely balls to the wall and hope Ray took the bait. It was a long shot but just might work. Besides, he really had nothing to lose.

After giving the bar the once over and sizing up any potential threats, Eric strolled behind Ray and stood opposite the register. His hand quickly disappeared behind his back, under his jacket. When it reappeared, nickel-plated chrome reflected the red neon sign above.

Ray's eyes bulged over the Taurus .357 revolver now aimed at the bartender's face.

"Give us all the cash," Eric said. "Slowly." Then to Ray, "Good call, man! There *is* a nice chunk of change here!"

Noticing the gun, the blue haired waitress shrieked like a cat with its tail under a rocker. The bartender jumped at the noise and slowly raised his hands. Some of the patrons turned to the commotion. Others ignored it and just sipped their beers.

"C'mon," Eric told Ray. "Handle crowd control as discussed."

"W-w-what the hell are you doing?" Ray asked, his voice a few octaves higher.

"Just what we talked about. Over at the table." Eric turned back to the bartender. "C'mon, old timer. I said give us the money."

The old man and Ray simultaneously said, "You serious?"

The hammer cocked on the pistol, rotating its cylinder. "What do you think?"

The old man went cross-eyed staring down the barrel.

Eric glanced over at his brother. "Okay, now's your chance to round up everyone's wallets like you've been wanting to."

Ray stood with his jaw unhinged over the turn of events. It made zero sense for Eric to do something so stupid. And, whatever his brother was trying to pull, Ray didn't want any part of it. "I'm outta here." He turned and made his way to the front door.

"Hey! Get back here! Don't puss out on me now, man."

Without turning, Ray flipped him the bird over his shoulder.

Eric glanced around to see if anyone was even buying his act anymore. "Yeah, good idea," he yelled back at Ray. "Go get the car ready. I'll handle this."

Pushing the door open, Ray held it and stepped aside to make way for the large, potbellied cowboy. The man nodded at the kind gesture while fumbling for the handkerchief in his rear pocket. Only a few steps into the bar, he shoved the cloth into his face and hunched over into a sneezing fit, his cowboy hat growing more crooked with each involuntary reflex.

All eyes were on the newcomer, jiggling, convulsing, screaming, and spraying into the handkerchief. Still holding the door open, Ray alternated glances between the cowboy, his brother, and the parking lot outside. Then he lowered his head and exhaled.

Noting Ray was staying put, Eric kept up the charade, thinking his brother might be coming around. He aimed his gun at the cowboy's back and waited for him to turn.

A half dozen sneezes later, the man—splotchy faced and watery eyed—slowly rose and noticed Ray blocking the closed front door. "Geez almighty," the cowboy said, adjusting his ten-gallon hat and shrugging his jacket back into place, "blasted ragweed is killin' my allergi—"

A whistle at the bar cut him off. The cowboy turned and saw the gun aimed at him.

"No! Don't!" Ray yelled at his brother.

Eric ignored him. "Yo, Sneezy. High five me. Both hands."

Before the cowboy could move, Ray rushed the man. He grabbed hold of his starched shirt and unleashed a flurry of blows. Being drunk, each shot was sloppy, but considering they were sucker punches, Ray managed to land a few that went a long way. The first punch to the face knocked the man's hat off. The second caught him in the gut and emptied his lungs. But it was the third that hit the magic button, right on the jaw. Knocked unconscious, the cowboy's knees unhinged and Ray eased him down to the ground, laying his fat belly across the sticky floor.

As Ray gasped for breath from the brief but powerful exchange, Eric came up beside him. "Damn, dude! Why'd you go all apeshit on the guy?"

Ray stooped, flipped up the tail of the cowboy's jacket, and snapped something from his back waistband. When he rose, Eric did a double take at the shiny Smith and Wesson .357 Magnum in Ray's hand.

"H-H-How ..." Eric said. "How did you know?"

Ray wedged a foot between the cowboy's fat belly and the dirty floor before flipping him over. He pointed at the man's waist. "There, jackass."

Clipped to the side of his leather belt, normally hidden by his front coat flaps, was a gold sheriff's deputy badge.

"Holy. Shit," Eric said. "You knew this guy was a—?"

"Small town, asshole," Ray said, nodding. "And you just royally fucked me."

Ray stared at the gun in his hands like it was a boil ready to burst. He quickly gave it to Eric then stormed past him and out the door.

A gun in each hand, Eric stood under the blue glow of a neon beer sign and admired the matching caliber revolvers. *Go figure. Just like a nice pair of gloves.* Getting back on the clock, he scanned the patrons and not a single eye met his until he looked at the bar.

The bartender extended a wad of cash. "You want this or not, young fella?"

Eric stared at the booty then quickly dismissed it with a wave of the hand. He might be an asshole, but he wasn't a goddamn asshole as to steal from some old bastard trying to earn a living.

"Nah," he said, shoving both pistols in his waistband. He retrieved a roll of cash from his pocket, snapped out three one hundred dollar bills, and threw them on the nearest table. "For the damages. And a round on me. For everyone."

For the first time that night, all eyes in the house turned to Eric, who was greeted with a half dozen near toothless grins. Eric shivered at the sight then pointed at the bartender. "Okay, now get over here and lock the door behind me. Got it?"

FOUR

STANDING AT HIS OLD, DENTED pickup truck, Ray frantically searched for its keys.

The Galaxie glided up behind him with engine chugging.

"What the hell?" Eric said, hanging out the driver's window. "You better get outta here, man."

Ray slapped his pockets like they were on fire. "Can't find my keys! Must've left 'em inside!" He spun and headed back to the bar.

The Galaxie shot in reverse and quickly caught up with him.

"Whoa-whoa-whoa, big guy!" Eric said. "*Don't* go in there. That cop might be awake now. And if that bartender has a gun stashed somewhere for protection, either might be itchin' to use it. C'mon. Hop in. I'll get ya outta here."

Stepping onto the porch, Ray reached for the handle to the front door then paused. It was obvious what might be waiting for him, leveled at his chest, if he walked back inside. He stood silent, only staring at Eric.

"C'mon, man," Eric said. He shoved open the passenger door, inviting Ray inside.

Ray shook his head, turned back to the bar, and pulled the handle.

The door didn't budge.

Although Eric knew it was locked, having heard the bartender turn over both bolts upon his exit, his heart still skipped a beat. His earlier warnings about the deputy regaining consciousness or the owner having a gun were not only valid but highly likely. Either party would probably be justified in using deadly force if Ray were to barge back inside.

Ray tried the front door again, but it still wouldn't give.

"C'mon!" Eric said. "I'm sure somebody's already called the cops. Which means you're fucked if you don't get in here." He smacked the passenger seat. "Now!"

Ray remained planted on the porch.

"Like you said ... small town. If you knew that cop, he probably knows of you and if not, I'll bet someone in there does and will be more than happy to rat you out for free beer."

Eric was right. Ray was a regular there. The bartender knew him. Maybe not by name, but by his face. And he'd worked a few construction gigs with some of the old timers in there. It wouldn't be hard for the cops to track him down.

"Fuck!" Ray exploded and kicked the rusted trash can beside him. It flew off the porch and landed on its side, spilling trash and roaches that scuttled for cover across the cracked asphalt.

"Oh, quit acting like a titty-baby and get your ass in here *now* before you get us both caught! What's done is done. And we got a job to do."

Running his hands through his hair, Ray paced the porch like a caged animal until ...

A siren rose in the distance.

Both men glanced in its direction.

Holy shit, Eric thought. *Could this be any more perfect?* "Get in!"

Ray stared back in defiance. Until his shoulders slumped.

As the approaching siren grew louder, the passenger door slammed shut. Then the Galaxie fishtailed out of the parking lot in a white cloud of smoke, taking its two passengers on a straight shot right into hell ...well before they'd ever have the chance to reach the Texas/Oklahoma state line.

FIVE

THE GOLDEN LIGHT FROM THE open glovebox cast a heavenly glow upon the pint of Jack Daniel's cradled within.

"Yes!" Ray said.

Eric always traveled with some sort of stash, but it was the fact that it was Quality Tennessee Whiskey and not some rot-gut that made Ray so goddamn giddy. He raked aside the insurance card and paperwork, letting them fall to the dark floorboard and get batted around by the whirlwind blowing in through the open windows.

"Ya mind?" Eric said, shaking his head as one of the documents got sucked out of the car. Granted, the paperwork was expired anyway, but that wasn't the point.

Ray ignored him and snatched up the whiskey bottle, broke its seal, and took a long draw.

"Take it easy with that shit."

"Ah, mind your own business."

"You're making it my business if ya start puking in my car." Eric reached for the bottle, but Ray pulled it away like a petulant child not wanting to share a toy.

Eric gripped the steering wheel tight and fought the urge to bust him one across the chops. Knowing his brother's high alcohol tolerance and how much of a pain in the ass he could be when drunk, it was going to be a very long night. Damn it, why didn't he think to remove the booze from the glovebox beforehand? A sober, pissed-off Ray was a lot easier to deal with than a drunk, pissed-off one.

Ray took another hearty gulp of alcohol.

"Hey, man. Slow down a bit, huh?"

"Fuck you."

Eric bit his tongue and checked the rearview. A few minutes passed before he spoke again. "Look, for what it's worth, thanks for handling the cop back there."

"Yeah, some things never change. Apparently ya still need me to wipe your ass for you."

"I'm thanking ya, dickhead. I realize you didn't have to get involved but I'm grateful ya did."

"Like I had a choice."

"I didn't ask you to knock out that cop."

"You're right. I should've just stepped aside and let you two go at it. See who'd get shot first."

"I had him covered."

"And what if he panicked? Gone for his gun?"

"Then whose fault would that be?"

"You don't get it, do you? What's fucked up is I still don't know whose life I felt was more important to save. Yours. Or his."

"Well, if that's where we stand, how 'bout I just drop you off at the next exit? I'm sure you can hitch a ride back to whatever rock you've been hiding under. Hell, forget hitching. I'll give ya cab fare. Next exit. How about it?"

"Drop me off?" Ray shook his head. "I can't go home, ya asshole! I just beat the shit out of a sheriff's deputy.

"Oh, c'mon, let's not be so dramatic."

"I did it in front of a half dozen witnesses!"

Eric shrugged. No argument there. He checked the rearview again.

"I stole his gun …"

"No. You relieved him of it." Eric patted the Smith and Wesson wedged in his waistband. "I stole it."

"Was an accessory to an armed robbery …"

"I didn't take the cash. In fact, I paid them for the damages. Damages that you caused, mind you."

Ray threw his hands up. "What's wrong with you? My pickup is sitting in the parking lot of that bar right now, probably swarming with cops that've just run my plates. With my two priors and the goddamn three-strikes law, I could get life for this shit!"

"Ya know, you're right! I *don't* understand. I'm giving you a gift and you—"

"Oh, please. Some gift!"

"It's called closure, asshole. And judging by the way I found you tonight, you need it. Running off to some bum-fuck town to drink yourself to death isn't what most would call—"

Ray exploded and punched the dashboard. "Christ! Would you shut up?! Just! Shut! Up!"

"Hey!" Eric reached over and ran his hand over the dash to make sure it wasn't damaged.

Ray jabbed a finger at him. "Just shut your mouth and leave me alone." He took another gulp of whiskey. "Why couldn't you have just forgotten about me?" Leaning back in his seat, Ray gazed into the darkness outside the passenger window. "Why …?"

The hum of the engine and the tires spinning across asphalt filled the awkward silence between the brothers. Leaving Ray alone was the best thing to do right now. Let him drink, pass out, and sober up since he was now in it for the long haul. Eric had won this battle but still had a long way to go to win the war. It was best to relish the small victory in silence. He turned back to the road and stared into the void beyond the headlights.

Thirty minutes had crawled by. In that time, Eric reassured himself what he was doing was the best thing for his brother. The right thing. Sure, he'd cornered Ray until his back was against the wall, but by doing so, he got him to come out fighting. And that is what Eric needed right now. He glanced over to see how the champ was holding up.

Slumped in the passenger seat, Ray turned up the pint and swallowed the last of the whiskey. The bottle fell to the dark floorboard with a loud clank. He belched up something juicy, swallowed it back down in disgust, and leaned his weary head against the side window. His heavy lids drooped and finally sealed shut. Baby had his bottle, was burped, and ready for his nap.

Eric breathed a sigh of relief. He checked his gauges on the glowing dash. The gas tank was over three quarters full. Engine temperature read normal. He shifted in his seat to test his bladder. No discomfort, so there wasn't a need to stop for a piss break that would only wake up Baby. Nope. It should be easy sailing from here on out ... at least for the next couple hours.

Ten minutes later a groan came from the passenger side. Ray squirmed in the seat. A thick sheen of sweat covered his pallid face. His breathing was short. Fast. His cheeks puffed and his mouth watered, lubricating what was about to come up.

"Oh, shit ..." Eric said. "No! No! Not in the car! Not in my car!"

The Galaxie skidded to a stop along the shoulder of the deserted highway. Eric quickly leaned across Ray and wrenched open the passenger door. "Get outta here!" He shoved Ray out to land on his hand and knees.

Like a frightened cat, Ray arched his back, sucking stomach to spine, and let loose a foamy projectile that splashed both his hands and the asphalt.

Relieved over the close call, Eric killed the engine and flipped off the lights to maintain stealth along the dark strip of highway. He grabbed an old t-shirt off the rear floorboard and approached his brother, tossing the cloth on the ground beside him. "Clean yourself up."

Groaning, Ray snatched it up and wiped his mouth. Even with his gut now half empty, the man was still shit-faced from all the alcohol his body had already absorbed. Ray slowly rose with knees buckling like an infant taking its first step. Eric placed a firm hand on his back to stop his swaying and guided him forward, propping him up against the Galaxie. Ray slumped over the car and laid his sweaty forehead against the cool metal roof. He let out a long groan of relief.

"Feel better?" Eric said.

As if touching a live wire, Ray sprung erect. He threw an arm over Eric's shoulder for support and leaned in way too close. Once his eyes were able to uncross and somewhat focus, he whispered, "Should've just left me alone ..." The words came out slurred like something delivered by a Bowery bum from an old black and white movie.

Eric winced at his puke breath and pushed him a step back.

In the distance, a pair of headlights pierced the darkness.

Was it best to get Ray in the car immediately? Or have him stay put? Hide behind it until the vehicle passed? Sure, the latter was easier, but if it turned out to be a cop, they'd have zero chance of escape just standing on the side of the road like two idiots.

"Get in the car," Eric said. "C'mon. Move it!" He opened the passenger door. Ray resisted, first squirming then pushing back in an attempt to break free.

"Stop being an asshole!" Eric said. Sober and stronger, he grabbed Ray and almost had him lined up to shove inside when his foot slid in the puddle of vomit. Eric's leg went out from under him and he narrowly avoided landing in the pool of puke.

Ready to pulverize Ray, he looked up and saw his brother shambling away, behind the car. Then his stomach dropped when he caught a glimpse of moonlight glinting off something metallic in Ray's hand. A heartbeat later, Ray was gone, moving in the direction of the road.

Eric reached behind his back to check for his gun. "Ohhh … shit."

Ray was already in middle of the highway, one hand waving the vehicle down, the other pointing Eric's pistol high above his head. He screamed at the headlights barreling toward him. "Hey!"

The vehicle failed to slow down, either not seeing the crazy drunk in its path or, quite the opposite, spotting a madman in the middle of the road holding a gun. Eric raced after his brother before he became roadkill.

The muzzle flashed and a loud crack sounded. Eric lurched back and skidded to a stop.

"Hey! Over here!" Ray waved at the headlights blasting his body. He squeezed off two more rounds straight up into the night sky, hoping for the driver's attention.

Tires squealed. The engine roared. And the minivan whipped around Ray, narrowly missing him. The blur of a woman's face— her mouth twisted in a scream of terror—flashed in the passenger window. In the blink of an eye, the vehicle blew by, causing his clothes to violently flap around him like a flag caught in the path of a tornado. The burst of wind knocked his drunk ass off balance. He spun and hit the ground then accidentally squeezed off a wild round. The bullet's high-pitched ricochet echoed into the night.

Once the bright red taillights disappeared over the hill, Eric popped up from behind the Galaxie, bug-eyed and hands waving. "Idiot! You-you-you goddamn moron!"

Ray groaned and rolled over to see Eric rushing at him. "Ahhh … shit …"

"What the fuck is wrong with you!" He snatched up his gun, grabbed Ray by the shirt collar, and yanked him to his feet. Ray stumbled on rubbery limbs as Eric dragged him across the pavement.

"What were you thinking?!"

"Sick of you. Just trying to get a ride. Trying to get their attention …"

Eric threw him in the passenger seat. "Congratulations! You certainly did that, all right!" Rolling up the passenger window, he kicked Ray's legs into the car. "Now they'll report some crazy guy in the middle of the highway shooting at them."

"Wasn't shooting at 'em. Just in the air. To get their attention."

"When they report it, the cops will know the way we're headin'."

"How they gonna know?"

"Think about it, stupid. Point A is where we held up the bar. You being Quick-Draw McGraw just gave them point B. Now they'll be waiting further down the road at point C."

Ray held up a finger. "Wait. Wait a minute. Just hold on. I thought you said we didn't hold up that bar."

Eric slammed the door in his face, momentarily sealing off the drunken stupidity.

Good God, what a cluster fuck, Eric thought. He walked to the rear of the car and leaned on its trunk, hoping to clear his mind and figure out what to do next. He stuck his hands in his jacket pocket and felt the set of keys. Ray's truck keys. After stealing a glance over his shoulder to make sure he wasn't being watched, he took them out and studied them. Then slowly exhaled. It was best to get rid of the evidence before it came back and bit him on the ass. Without hesitating, he hurled them into the pitch black field beside them.

All right, now what? Get back on track. Focus.

If the people in the minivan caught the make and model of his car and reported it, then the authorities just might have an eager cop waiting somewhere up ahead. So it might be best to get off the interstate and—

The muffler exploded between his legs and the engine roared to life.

"Oh, no-no-no-no-no!" he said, running to the driver's side and ripping open the door. Terrified to find his drunk brother behind the wheel, ready to peel off down the road without him, Eric thankfully saw Ray still in the passenger seat, only fiddling with the knobs on the temperature control.

"Cold," he said, shivering. It was far from chilly outside, but the alcohol in his system had thinned the man's blood. "How does the damn heat work?"

Swallowing his heart back to his chest, Eric climbed behind the wheel and slapped Ray's hand away from the dials. He flipped on the heat and aimed a vent at his brother to shut him up. Once hit by the blast of warmth, Ray grinned and leaned back in his seat.

While Eric pulled out his phone and fiddled with his GPS, Ray crossed his arms and closed his eyes. Within seconds, the man was snoring.

Eric looked out the windshield and back to his phone. He nodded and set the cell beside him on the seat.

Then the Galaxie glided back onto the highway and, moments later, its taillights sunk over the inky horizon.

SIX

HER BLOOD APPEARED BLACK in the moonlight. Each inky dot peppering the tile entryway reflected the full moon shining through the open front door.

The light in the foyer didn't work. Ray stared into the house, facing a complete wall of black. He raised the tire iron slightly higher in case someone was hiding there, waiting to attack. He tried the switch again, clicking it back and forth, and a chill slithered up his spine.

Dear God, Ray thought, *please,* please *let her be all right.*

He had received a call only forty minutes earlier from Donna, Rachel's friend and coworker at the diner. When Donna came in for her night shift, she was told by the other waitstaff Rachel had failed to show up earlier for her swing swift. No call, no show, and totally out of character. Donna knew Rachel would never blow off a shift, especially with the money problems she and Ray were having lately. She called Rachel's cell but kept getting her voicemail. Text messages went unanswered. And when she tried her at home, the answering machine never picked up. That's when the sinking in her gut told her to call Ray at the garage to see what was up.

Hearing Donna's words over the phone, Ray broke out in a cold sweat and bolted out of the auto repair shop without informing his boss.

His calls to both the home phone and Rachel's cell also went unanswered. Expecting trouble, he called Eric and told him to meet him at the house. And to come armed.

Ray immediately suspected Jacobs. The man was nothing but a piece of shit from day one, but they needed a third guy for the job. Big mistake. During the robbery, Jacobs started in with a young, blond hostage, wanting to take her in back for a few minutes instead of watching the front door. When Ray and Eric objected and told him to get back on the clock, he unzipped his pants and removed her gag for something a little quicker and on the spot. That's when Ray knocked him out cold, flat on his ass. The only reason they didn't leave him for the cops was the high probability he'd rat them out to save his own tail. So they dragged him to the car, threw him in, and dropped his unconscious ass off with a mutual friend ... minus his third of the cut he failed to earn. Now, almost a week later, he must have grown a huge pair, showing up at Ray's place looking for his piece of the pie or, worse, to leave a calling card he was not to be messed with.

Managing to hit every red light along the way, Ray finally pulled up to his house and found it dark, silent. Rachel's car was still in the driveway.

An icy hand clamped over his heart. Snatching the tire iron from under his seat, he rushed up the walkway and pushed open the front door left ajar. He paused and stared into the shadowy house, barely able to distinguish the strange shapes of his own living room.

"Rachel?" he called out, trying the light switch.

Ray stepped forward and broken glass crunched underfoot. His eyes slowly adjusted and he saw the drops of blood on the linoleum floor.

"Rachel!"

Heart hammering in his chest, he rushed forward into the darkness for the switch on the opposite side of the living room. *It's okay*, he tried to reassure himself. *Just a random break-in. Neighborhood punks. They just scared her away. That's all. She's probably safe. Over at the neighbors.*

But he knew it was much worse.

"Honey, it's me. Are you here?"

The knot in his stomach slid tighter. He continued forward, careful not to bark his shin on the coffee table that should've been somewhere to his left. His feet slid across the carpet until his boot stopped against what felt like a mound of wet laundry.

He froze when the obstruction moved against his foot. A moist gurgle sounded. And when his name was called in an agonizing whisper, his worst fear became reality.

Ray fell to his knees and felt sticky, cold flesh under his trembling fingers.

"Ra-Rachel?" he whimpered.

The approaching roar of the Galaxie's engine broke the silence outside. As the car skidded to a stop, its headlights blasted through the open front door, shedding light into the room.

Ray saw the full extent of carnage and howled in horror.

Eric entered the front door with gun drawn and saw his brother kneeling in a pool of blood, rocking the broken, naked body of his wife. The room around them was completely upended. Ransacked.

"Jacobs ..." whispered Eric, squeezing the pistol tight.

Ray looked up at Eric in desperation, pleading for reassurance that this wasn't real. That Rachel was fine and somewhere else. And this swollen, bruised, destroyed body in his arms belonged to someone else.

Rachel gasped and reached for his hand. He took it and almost pulled back in horror. One of her fingers—her index finger—was missing. Cut off. Warm blood dribbled out of the wound like a leaking faucet and ran down his chest, spreading across his lap. A gurgle rattled its way up her crushed throat and out the bloody mouthful of broken teeth. Ray stared at her, waiting for her to speak, unable to see her beautiful brown eyes through their swollen lids.

Then her body gave out and she went limp.

"No-no-no-no-no-no-no. Oh, God! No!" Desperate, Ray gave her a gentle shake, as if to jolt her back into consciousness. There was no response. Knowing why, he opened his mouth and unleashed a silent scream.

Ray snapped awake. He squinted and slapped down the car visor to shield his eyes from the morning sun blasting through the Galaxie's windshield. His head felt like it was pinned in a vice by some sadist who was getting his rocks off by slowly tightening it. Through slitted lids, he glanced next to him, saw a fuzzy version of his brother driving, and quickly turned away. "Not a word," he whispered, rubbing his aching temples.

Last night was a near blank, at least after getting into Eric's car. But he did remember what was important: the envelope of directions. His birthday gift. He also remembered losing his truck keys. Eric holding up the bar. Him beating the deputy—Hank, he thought the guy's name was—before any shots could be fired. And, finally, without a choice, climbing into the Galaxie for the long trip north. Once again, it seemed whenever Eric popped up, things went straight to hell. The last time happening three years ago, when he showed up at their doorstep with a promise of easy money at a low risk ...

Ray groaned. Dehydrated, he licked his chapped lips. His body was in desperate need of a gallon of water and a half bottle of aspirin. Eyes closed, he leaned back and pressed his burning forehead against the door window, wincing every time he bumped its hard surface from the unsteady road. "Can we stop?" Ray said. "Get some water?"

A quick grunt came from the driver's side.

The car rattled. Outside the passenger window, the rural landscape inched closer, creeping in on the Galaxie. The vehicle continued vibrating then went smooth as it moved off the bumpy shoulder and back onto the paved road. The commotion made Ray slowly open his eyes and take a peek under the sun visor.

The interstate was gone, now replaced by an isolated, two-lane road bordered by open fields and sprinkled with a few dead trees. A deep ravine snaked along the right side of the road.

Where the hell were they? And *why* were they there?

Ray craned his neck and peered over into the dirt ravine. On average, it ran about twenty-five feet wide and fifteen feet deep. Staring into the winding crevice as it whipped by caused his head to spin and stomach to tighten. He turned forward to avoid throwing up.

Through the windshield, the yellow dividing line on the road was slowly creeping under the car. The vehicle was moving into the opposite lane. Ray flipped up the visor and his eyes shot wide open. Although there was no oncoming traffic, there was something equally formidable ahead—a very large oak tree planted on the opposite side of the road ... and the Galaxie was barreling directly for it.

"Hey!" Ray turned to Eric, whose head was lowered and eyes closed. "Shit! Wake up!" Ray grabbed the wheel in an attempt to steer the vehicle back on course.

Eric sprung awake and lurched forward but his seatbelt caught him and threw him back. His eyes practically popped from their sockets at the sight of the tree racing at them. He jerked the wheel to the right. Overcorrected. Stomped the brakes.

The tires locked. After a deafening squeal of rubber over asphalt, the Galaxie shot off the road, plowed through a thin barrier of brush, and flew into the dirt ravine.

"Jesus Chr—!" Eric screamed. "Hold on!"

The car rocketed into the opposite side of the embankment. With the deafening sound of crunching metal, the jarring impact shot them forward until their safety belts snapped them back in place. A wave of dirt crashed over both hood and windshield and blocked out the sun. The momentum lifted the Galaxie's rear end to a forty-five-degree angle, balancing the vehicle on its nose. Both men braced the dash. Then the rear of the car went into freefall and their stomachs dropped along with it. The vehicle slammed flat, its bumper wedging itself into the opposite wall of the ravine. After a near spine-shattering bounce, the Galaxie finally went still. With the engine chugging and fighting to stay alive, smoke billowed in through the air vents, adding to the choking dust already filling the car's interior.

SEVEN

GROANING, ERIC PUT THE CAR in park and slid his foot off the brake. It fell to the floor with a heavy thud.

Ray was hunched forward, cradling his throbbing head. After a moment, he noticed the smoke creeping around them. "Kill the engine. Now!"

Unable to move, Eric stared blankly at him. The shock of totaling his car was all consuming. Ray gave him a shake, but he still didn't act.

Before the Galaxie caught fire, Ray leaned over and flipped the keys in the ignition. The engine chugged, rattled, and finally died. An eerie silence floated over them as the dust settled.

"You okay?" Ray said.

Eric finally snapped out of it. "No! My car!"

The men opened their doors and looked down at the ground—a good four feet below. With the Galaxie's crumpled hood partially devoured by one side of the embankment and its rear bumper resting on the other, the vehicle sat wedged between the two slopes, its tires failing to touch earth.

The brothers carefully slid out to assess the damage.

After taking in the entire scene, Eric shook his head in disbelief. The only way the car was getting out was by wrecker. And even then it wasn't going anywhere with its broken axle.

Ray shambled to a large rock, sat down, and lowered his pounding head into his hands.

"Fuuuck," Eric said. "She's a goner." Stretching his arms over the car's front quarter panel and hood, he lowered his head and gave her a final hug like bidding farewell to a beloved pet about to be euthanized. "I'm so sorry, baby."

Ray rose and climbed the embankment to check out the road. As previously seen, it was eerily deserted. Zero signs of life, not even a stretch of telephone wire or a satellite tower. He swallowed hard and yearned for that gallon of water even more so now.

Scraping away enough dirt to pop the trunk, Eric climbed into the vehicle's spacious cargo area and rummaged through a couple of tightly packed duffle bags.

"Where are we?" Ray asked.

Eric glanced up at his brother, who stood on the edge of the ravine. He ignored the question and went back to the contents of the trunk.

"Hey. What are we doing out here?"

"Well, what we are doing out here is keeping a low profile. Especially after some drunk jackass was firing a gun at people on the highway last night."

It took a minute for the fog to slowly lift. Then, "Oh, shit. I-I kinda remember ... Please tell me no one got hurt."

"Hurt? No. Fucked? Yes. As in us. Because of your ass, we had to take this little detour to avoid a much easier and more direct route." He pulled a bottle of aspirin out of a bag and tossed it up to his brother.

Ray caught it and carefully descended the slope. Each step sent a mini-avalanche of dirt tumbling across his path. Stopping halfway down the embankment, he sat next to the trunk, popped open the bottle, and chewed a few aspirin. "So *where* are we?"

"Well, I know we passed some town called Penumbra before sunrise. That's the last road sign I saw before losing my cell signal and the GPS crapped out." Eric pulled out a one-liter water bottle from a bag. "Well, lookee here. Knew I had this in here somewhere." Seeing the water, Ray's eyes lit up like a cat hearing a can opener. "It's left over from the last time I was at the gym." He tossed it to Ray. "Bottle might smell like sweaty socks but what's inside should be fine."

Greedily gulping down half of it, Ray moaned and wiped his mouth with the back of his sleeve. He recapped the water and offered both it and the aspirins back to Eric, who waved him off.

"Keep 'em. You need them more than me." Eric pulled out a set of pocket binoculars from another bag, gave them the once over, and tucked them into his jacket.

A silence fell over the area. Both men looked around, trying to gauge their next step.

"Did you try backtracking once you lost the signal?" Ray said.

"Yep. And I must've taken a wrong turn somewhere."

"So we're lost." A statement, not a question.

"Looks like it, huh?" Eric grabbed a duffle bag and tossed it out of the trunk. The bag landed next to Ray with a heavy thud and a jingle of brass. Ray scooted slightly away from it like it was a giant tarantula that just scuttled up beside him. He knew what it contained—ammunition.

Eric held up a pump-action shotgun and shook his head. "Just got this. Was hoping to break it in," he glanced up toward the road, "but given our current predicament, it's kinda hard to look inconspicuous walking around with it, huh?" The shotgun got tossed back into the trunk.

"So what now?" Ray asked.

It appeared the ravine they crashed in snaked alongside the road for quite a while. Traveling it would keep them out of sight but still close enough to hear any approaching vehicles. Until then, they'd walk. Keep moving. The clock was ticking. "We follow this," Eric said, pointing his chin up the ravine. "Wait for someone to come along. Then get us a new set of wheels."

Ray shot him a look. "You mean hitch a ride, right?"

"Sure. Whatever." Eric grinned, climbed out of the trunk, and went to the bag of ammo. "Anyway, that's my plan. But now that you've sobered up, the more important question is … what's yours?"

A long beat. Ray scratched his chest and shrugged. "I got nowhere to go."

"Sure you do. To Oklahoma. With me."

"No. Once we get out of …" he looked around, "wherever *here* is, we go our separate ways."

"You just said ya got nowhere to go. So what're you gonna do? Wander around the country like The Incredible Hulk on that old TV show?"

"Better than what you've got planned."

Eric threw down the bag of ammo. "Why are you fighting me on this?! I really don't get it!"

"And you wouldn't, even if I tried to explain it. I'm done. And I'm not going back. No matter the reason. No matter how much you think I should. I buried all that shit when I buried my wife." Ray continued to scratch at his chest. It wasn't sore from the seatbelt. He just needed to feel what hung around his neck to calm the rising sickness in his gut.

Eric waited for him to continue. For something—anything— that might explain why his brother was going to allow the bastard responsible for the torture and murder of his wife to continue breathing the same air they did. It didn't make a lick of sense that he'd become so spineless in such a short period of time. Then, it hit him. Though he was terrified of the answer, he had to ask, "You find God or something?"

Ray scoffed and rose to his feet. Turning away, he silently stared off into the distance.

There really wasn't time for this. Eric took a half box of .357 ammo from the bag and shoved it into his coat pocket. He didn't expect to need it, but it'd be stupid not to take it because of the cops … and that little extra something he still needed to tell Ray about.

But all in due time.

Standing halfway up the bank, Ray watched the weeds along the ravine's edge sway in a synchronized dance choreographed by the wind. The movement was hypnotic. Peaceful.

"Here," came from over his shoulder.

Turning, Ray saw Eric offering him a pistol.

"Just in case," Eric said.

Ray dismissed it with a shake of his head then descended to the bottom of the ravine.

Growling, Eric shoved the extra gun into his waistband. "Fine. It'll be here if you need it." He threw the bag of ammo back into the trunk, locked it, then followed his brother, who was already leading the way through the winding gorge.

About a half mile up, Eric stopped cold and patted his various pockets.

Ray gave him an inquisitive look.

"My cell," Eric said, glancing back in the direction of the car. "Shit."

"Fine. I'll wait here."

"You leave yours?"

"Ain't got one."

Eric asked, incredulously, "You don't have a cell phone anymore?"

Ray shrugged. "Who the hell am I gonna call?"

Eric opened his mouth to say something along the lines of *How about me? Your brother, ya asshole?* but thought better of it. Now wasn't the time. He simply turned and headed back to the car without another word.

While Eric backtracked through the snaking ravine, Ray sat upon a large rock, popped another aspirin, and finished the water. It was foolish to drink it all, especially not knowing how long it might be before they'd cross paths with someone, but getting rid of his alcohol dehydration took precedent.

Leaning forward, he clasped his hands together and looked down at the early morning sunlight reflecting off his gold wedding band. He polished it with his opposite thumb then quickly covered it.

Maybe it was time to check out the road above. Maybe the short distance already traveled offered a new vantage point of a gas station or farmhouse up ahead. Ray climbed the embankment and stood within the waist-high weeds along the road. Though his head still felt as tight as an overinflated tire, the gentle breeze and warm sun felt good across his face.

A flash of reflecting sunlight in the distance caught his attention. It came from the direction of their wreck site. He squinted and made out the approaching vehicle. Then his heart leaped to his throat.

It was a police cruiser.

EIGHT

RAY DROPPED FOR COVER WITHIN the brush and saw the cop car approaching their accident scene. He scanned the ravine for Eric, couldn't find him, then looked back at the cruiser closing in. If the cop was paying even the slightest attention to the road, he'd spot the skid marks that ripped through the flattened brush at the edge of the ravine and stop to investigate a possible accident.

Ray cupped his hands to his face and yelled, "Eric! Cop!" He was about to scream louder, but figured it best to stop standing there shouting like an idiot and just go get his brother before the cop spotted him. He scuttled back through the weeds and dropped down the embankment, trying to avoid kicking up a dust cloud that might signal his activity. With heart pounding, he raced through the winding ravine, whipping around each blind curve to reach Eric before it was too late. Rushing out of a narrow pathway and into the larger area that contained the wrecked Galaxie, a hand shot out from his blind spot, grabbed his shirt collar, and wrenched him back—nearly off his feet. Eric caught his brother and pulled him upright.

"Quiet," Eric whispered, pointing to the edge of the ravine, just above the Galaxie. He was already privy to their visitor.

Squeaking brake pads echoed from above.

Eric ticked his head opposite the Galaxie and Ray nodded in agreement. It was time to get the hell out of there. Now.

The brothers raced for cover deep within the winding ravine before a car door opened and a shadow from atop the embankment stretched over the wrecked Galaxie.

"Think they got an APB on us?" Eric asked, spying through the binoculars.

The brothers were dug in deep within the thick overgrowth and watched the parked cruiser down the road with its flashing cherries on top. Before Ray could attempt an answer, the officer scrambled out of the ravine with pistol drawn while speaking into his shoulder mic. Gun at the ready, his head whipped back and forth, scanning his surroundings like a spooked owl. Once at the cruiser, he holstered his piece in exchange for the much larger shotgun from the front mount. He pumped it once to rack a shell then continued with radioing in his find.

"Guess so," Eric said grimly. "C'mon. Let's get outta here before backup arrives."

Walking for hours in silence, they listened for any approaching vehicles, police or otherwise, but heard nothing. Behind them were cops, and in front ... who the hell knew?

It was best to keep moving and find another set of wheels before the police picked up their trail. Of course, it wasn't like they were on the most wanted list, but assaulting the cop back at the bar and stealing his gun had put a little heat on them, something they could do without.

As they continued on, the only sounds heard were the wind rustling the fields above and the crunch of earth underfoot. The ravine grew shallower, eventually leveling off and spitting them out into an open prairie. Ray and Eric cautiously stepped out to check their surroundings. The road they assumed was next to them was now gone, replaced by more open grasslands.

"What the …?" Eric said. He quickly fished the binoculars out of his pocket and scanned the horizon.

The ravine must have gradually distanced itself from the road without them realizing it. Maybe they should've climbed the embankment a little more often to check their progress. But it was too late now.

"Okay … so what's the plan?" Ray asked. "Head back? Find the road and stick to it?"

Backtracking was a waste of time, something they didn't have the luxury of. Eric turned to the open field in front of them. A gradual treeline formed in the distance. Beyond it might be a farmhouse or two. The evidence of that possibility being a single lane dirt road leading into the woods. He used the binoculars for a closer look.

The road was recently traveled, its surface lined with tire tracks now baked into the earth after the heavy rains the southern part of the state received only a few days ago.

"We go forward," Eric said. "That road's bound to lead somewhere."

"It's no wider than a damn driveway."

"And tell me, Einstein, what do driveways lead to?"

Ray gave their newfound destination the once over. Besides the road, the field in front of them showed no evidence of civilization. Which probably meant it only led deeper into the sticks.

"C'mon," Eric said. "We follow it but keep to the woods for cover."

"Just like the great job we did using the ravine?"

"We'll pay better attention," Eric snapped. "Give it few miles.

See if it opens up somewhere or gives us a better view of where we are. If we don't see anything, we turn back."

Ray gave an unsure look.

"We gotta at least fuckin' try," Eric said. "We already know there ain't shit back there." He thumbed over his shoulder. "So, c'mon." He started for the treeline.

Ray scanned the horizon once more and followed his brother.

Keeping a close eye on the road, they walked in silence for a few miles until Ray's curiosity got the best of him. "Tell me," he said, "ya got more access to firepower for when you reach this guy in Oklahoma? 'Cause if he's got buddies, you'll need more than two revolvers and a box of bullets."

"Actually, I got a little less than half a box of bullets right now."

"I'm serious."

"Don't worry. I've got a contingency plan."

They continued on. Ray chewed another aspirin and waited for Eric to elaborate. When he didn't, Ray chomped at the bit. "So? What is it?"

"What's what?"

"Your contingency plan?"

"You remember Fatty McPhattens?"

Ray chuckled. "How could I forget that fat bastard? He still running that fleabag motel outside of Fort Worth?"

"Yep. He's alive and jiggling in Funky Town. Lets me use one of his rooms for storage. Got all we need waiting there. And then some. We can stop on the way. That is, once we find ourselves a new car."

Ray scoffed. "What's all this *we* shit?"

Eric ignored him.

"I'm serious. You do understand that I'm not—"

Holding up his hand, Eric halted in his tracks and motioned for Ray to do the same. Ray glanced over to where his brother was pointing and saw movement up ahead between the trees. Both men crouched then went for a closer look.

NINE

STANDING ALONE IN AN AREA sparsely populated by
trees, a man in his late sixties was packing the loose earth at his
feet with a shovel. An empty burlap bag sat on the ground beside
him. After giving the soil a final whack, he stood erect, winced, and
rubbed his lower back. Leaning on the tool, he pulled a handkerchief from his ratty overalls, blew his nose in it, and, without turning
it over, used the snotty cloth to wipe the sweat from his face and
bald head.

The brothers grimaced over the unsanitary act.

The man snatched the burlap sack from the ground then started
for the thicket of trees in the opposite direction.

Once he disappeared, Ray and Eric stealthily pursued him, weaving around trees while using them as cover. The man approached an
orange pickup truck with an oversized, white aluminum camper
stuck on its bed like a gorged ivory tick.

"Bingo," Eric whispered.

The man tossed the shovel through the open passenger window
and made his way around the front of the truck.

Eric took a step forward and Ray grabbed his shoulder to stop him.

"We're just asking for a ride, right?" Ray said. "Nothing more?"

"Ya really think that piece of shit could get us all the way up to Oklahoma? I *ain't* stealing it. You stealing it?"

"Good. Then we have an understanding. No more trouble."

"Ummm ... weren't you the one shooting at people on the highway last night?"

Ray bit his lip.

Eric patted his shoulder. "Yeah, that's what I thought. C'mon."

The old man opened the driver's door. As he was about to climb in behind the wheel, "Hey, there," came from over his shoulder.

The man nearly leaped out of his ratty work boots and spun around. "Jesus H!" He clutched his chest with a palsied grip and fell back against the truck, feigning a heart attack.

The brothers retreated a few steps toward the camper and raised their hands in mock surrender.

"Easy there, old timer," Eric said.

The man shook his head and exhaled. "What the hell ya'll doin' out here?!"

"We had an accident a few miles back," Eric replied.

"Well, ya damn near made me have one right here in my britches, sneakin' up on me like that!"

While his brother talked to the man, Ray checked out the truck. He stepped closer to one of the camper's plexiglass windows, curious for a peek inside.

"Well, we didn't mean to scare ya," Eric continued. "But as I was saying, we got in a wreck. Swerved to avoid hitting an armadillo and—"

"Nasty critters. Them carry leprosky, ya know?"

"Leprosy, too."

The man seemed momentarily perplexed before realizing he was being made fun of. Still, he let it go and looked around impatiently. "Accident, huh? Well ... sucks to be you. Then again, you seem like a smart fellow, so I'm sure you'll figure something out."

Ray saw the situation going south fast. He knew it was best to handle it himself if they wanted to get a ride out of there. Before he could intervene, movement in the camper's window caught his eye. He inched forward for a closer look.

"Have a nice one, boys." The old man turned to the open cab.

"Wait," Eric said. "We thought maybe you could give us a ride to—"

The man spun with a shit-eating grin. "Well, ya thought wrong. Guess you ain't so smart after all. Huh?"

Those revolvers tucked in Eric's back waistband were just itching to come out for a little fresh air and sunshine. If the old timer wasn't so up there in years, he'd pistol whip the son-of-a-bitch and teach him some manners. Instead, he vetoed the gun and decided to take a more pugilistic approach, one using his bare hands.

"Ya know," Eric responded. "I think it best you reconsider or maybe—"

A smiling face suddenly popped up in one of the camper windows. Ray gasped and lurched back.

Before Eric could finish his threat, Ray quickly hooked a hand on his brother's arm, spun him around, and nodded for him to look at the window.

Both stared at the young man in his early twenties crouching within the camper. He had a fresh shaved pate, a simpleton's wide-eyed expression, and a face split by a grin full of crooked teeth.

The old man noticed the younger one and slammed a fist against the camper. "Sit yer ass down, boy!"

The face darted back out of sight. The action made the truck rock and its shocks loudly creak. The old man turned back to the brothers. "Now what was that you was saying, son?" he asked Eric.

The game had changed. Before making any move to commandeer the truck, Eric needed to know how many others were in the camper. Until then, it was best to play it cool. "Ah, actually I was going to ask if you'd reconsider giving us a ride."

No response. The old man kept a good poker face.

"Maybe to the nearest gas station, sir," Ray added. "Or, even better, if there's a town nearby."

The man continued his stare, milking the uncomfortable silence for all its worth. Then he shook his head. "Nope. Don't think so. Got things to do." He moved for the cab.

"You can't just leave us out here," Eric said. "We don't even know where the hell we are."

"Should've thought of that before ya got lost."

Eric glanced at Ray and shrugged. "What the hell does that even mean?"

"Means," the man continued, sliding behind the wheel, "that you two boys are shit outta luck."

"Can you at least point us in the direction of I-35?" Ray said. "Or is it still I-69? Whichever is closer."

"Whichever is closer?" The man chuckled. "Boy, you *are* lost."

"All right." Eric stepped forward clenching a wad of bills. "We'll pay ya. For the ride." He snapped out a twenty and held it up.

The old man eyed the offering. "Twenty dollars, huh?" He thought about it, then: "Nope. Told ya I'm busy."

"Yeah," Eric said. "Guess digging holes in the middle of the woods can fill a whole day, huh?"

The old man's eyes narrowed at Eric. A real anger seemed to be brewing behind them.

Something about all this just didn't feel right to Ray. Here was a guy refusing to help someone claiming to have been in an accident. Stranded out there. And this joker wasn't interested in lifting a finger to help? Maybe he had something in the back of the truck he didn't want known. Something illegal. Ray glanced around, looking for smoke from something like a moonshine distillery or a meth lab vent poking out of the ground. It might be stretching things a bit, but still within reason since the rear passenger did look like a tweeker. Whatever the case, Ray knew they couldn't afford to lose the ride. The sooner they reached the nearest town, the sooner he and Eric could part ways.

The man slammed the driver's door shut and reached for the keys dangling in the ignition.

Ray grabbed the wad of cash from Eric. He'd seen a glint of greed in the man's eyes over the twenty and figured it just wasn't the right price. He pulled out four more twenties. "Hundred bucks. All yours. Just get us to an interstate."

The man stared at the bills and licked his chapped lips. Then he sized up Ray and Eric. "You two trouble?"

"No, sir," Ray answered. "Like we said, just had an accident and—"

"'Cause we don't want no trouble," the man continued. "No siree, don't like no trouble at all."

"Neither do we. We just wanna get back to the highw—"

Without warning, the man snatched the money from Ray.

"So we gotta deal?" Eric asked.

The man grunted and shoved the bills in the ashtray. "The name's Lew. Hop in back. Got too much shit up here."

Ray and Eric glanced across Lew and into the passenger seat covered with soiled, lumpy, burlap sacks. The sudden cross breeze over the bags assaulted their nostrils with a nauseating stench of something akin to week-old trash and dirty diapers. So maybe riding in back was for the best.

"Just never mind the boys," Lew said, ticking his head to the rear. The truck bounced then the tailgate dropped open.

The brothers glanced at the back of the truck.

"Thanks, Lew," Ray said then turned to Eric. "C'mon."

Eric hesitated halfway there and stopped. "Ya know how I hate tight spaces."

Ray caught Lew watching them in the side mirror. He quickly positioned himself to block the old man's view. "I know," Ray whispered. "You're just gonna have to tough it out. This could be our only ride out of here."

Eric nodded slightly and Ray put a hand on his shoulder for both reassurance and to guide him to the rear of the truck. All seemed well until they turned the corner and saw what waited for them inside the camper.

"Oh, you *gotta* be fuckin' kidding me," Eric said.

TEN

TWO MEN IN THEIR EARLY twenties, both with shaved heads, sat within the cramped confines of the truck bed. The thin, lanky one—glimpsed earlier in the window—was the very definition of squirrelly. The left shoulder of his dirty t-shirt was stained wet. He shook his head and tried to speak but a spasm overtook his entire body like some uncontrollable chill. It was only after *licking* his shoulder twice that he regained control of his motor skills. Then he gave his shoulder another quick lick on the wet spot, hooted loudly, and waved.

Before Eric could turn to Ray and tell him abso-fucking-lutely *not*, the other fellow in the back—at least a buck-fifty overweight, wedged in a wheelchair, and wearing only a sweat-stained tank top and equally soiled whitey-tighties—swung his head in their direction and gave them the stink eye. With tongue poking out, the whipping motion threw a long strand of drool that dribbled onto his enormous gut, which was only half-covered by the tight shirt. One arm hung limply over the wheelchair's side while the other was wedged between his bruised, milky thighs like he was attempting to pick the underwear from his ass crack and got confused as to which way to go about it.

The camper's decor and degree of cleanliness rivaled that of its occupants. The bed was lined with dirty blankets and various trash—food wrappers, newspapers, soda cans, empty motor oil bottles. The pungent stench of body odor, urine, and feces attracted a swarm of flies.

The skinny fellow crawled closer for a formal introduction. "Hi. My name's Skeeter." Without missing a beat, he licked the wet spot on his shirt.

Ray and Eric eyed the guy's shoulder, clueless as to what it was that tasted so great.

"And this here's my brother TC." Skeeter licked himself again. "TC's not right in the head, but he's no retard." He did a double take at his fat, wheelchair-bound brother then glanced back at Ray and Eric and whispered, "Just don't sneeze in front of him. Sudden movements scare him."

Skeeter suddenly smashed his nose into his shoulder and gnawed at the wet spot like a dog going after a flea. The friction of his teeth gnashing against the fabric made a squeaking noise. TC shrieked and recoiled from the unexpected movement like Frankenstein's monster taking a torch to the face. The truck rocked, its shocks squeaked.

"Oops!" Skeeter said. He slowly reached out and cautiously rubbed TC's fat belly to calm him. After a moment, TC giggled and drooled, an obvious sign all was good.

In the cab, Lew spun around to the freak show taking place in back. He hit the window, jabbed a grimy finger at Skeeter, and screamed through the glass, his breath fogging its surface. "You shut your fuckin' hole before I come back there and blister yer ass!"

The glass might have muffled the threat, but Skeeter still heard it loud and clear. He scuttled away from the open tailgate and returned to the front of the bed, pressing his back against the driver's side corner.

TC seemed oblivious to the family squabble, finding the sight of the two strangers much more appealing.

"C'mon, boys!" Lew yelled at Ray and Eric through the glass. "Them won't bother ya no more." He flashed a smile, wiggled his bushy brows, and motioned for them to hop in.

Eric groaned and shook his head. "Nope. Not gonna happen." He quickly retreated from the open camper.

Ray gave chase. "Hey! Remember your out-of-town meeting?" he said, trying to keep his voice down.

"Yeah. Which is all the more reason we should cut the charade and just take the truck. Leave them here. By the time they get a chance to notify any cops, we'll be long gone."

"We don't know where the hell we are. Just taking off and driving blind like that could put us even deeper in the sticks. It's best we let the old guy get us somewhere first. Okay? Besides, you really wanna be responsible for abandoning him," Ray pointed his chin at TC, "out here on the side of the road?"

Eric paused a moment to take it into consideration.

"Really?" Ray said.

"Okay. Fine." Eric sighed. "But dibs on the tailgate."

The old man watched Ray and Eric from the rearview mirror as they made their way back to the truck.

Ray entered first, climbing in on his hands and knees. When Eric followed, his palm pressed into something soft and squishy hidden within the blanket's folds. He yanked his hand back as if touching a hot coil and groaned in disgust. Luckily, his palm was clean but he still gave it a few wipes on his pants leg for peace of mind.

Sitting cross-legged opposite Skeeter, Ray pressed his back firmly against the camper to keep his distance. Eric plopped down across from TC, where his view was a straight shot into the fat man's crotch. It wasn't clear if TC was sitting on his fingers or simply cupping his balls but Eric hoped that hand stayed put for the duration of the trip. The last thing needed was for the guy to take it out and wave it around after it'd been marinating in his own fromunda sweat. Trying to focus on the positive, Eric turned away and studied the beautiful scenery just outside the open tailgate.

With each pair of brothers lining a side of the bed, the pickup exploded to life and blew out a black cloud of exhaust that rolled back into the camper. Eric caught the blast first but had enough foresight to hold his breath and avoid choking on the toxic smoke. Ray waved the air to help disperse the exhaust. Skeeter glanced at TC then over at Ray and shook his head for him to stop. No sudden movements, remember? Ray slowly dropped his hand into his lap. He gave a couple closed mouth coughs and sat still.

Skeeter scuttled down the center of the bed to close the tailgate and practically crawled into Eric's lap in order to pass TC's beefy legs jutting from the wheelchair. Skeeter grabbed the edge of the gate and looked up at his brother. "Loud noise," he said then slammed the tailgate closed. TC lurched away from the noise and growled.

Ray and Eric exchanged a glance.

Skeeter grabbed the handle on the raised camper window and pulled it down, sealing them all inside.

"Whoa-whoa-whoa-whoa!" Eric said. "How about we leave that open, Slick? Get some fresh air in here."

Ray nodded. The tight quarters smelled like a combination of outhouse and locker room.

"Oh, no! No can do," Skeeter said. He ticked his head at TC. "He'll freak if that window stays open." He leaned in closer to Eric and whispered with breath that smelled like he'd been nibbling shit, "That's how TC got that way. Fell out on his head when he was lil' and tumbled for a good quarter mile before anyone noticed him gone."

Both Ray and Eric looked over at TC, at his frozen expression and blank gaze.

Eric shook his head and muttered, "God … just our luck."

"Lucky you are, my friend," Skeeter said. "'Cause we don't normally give people rides. Especially strangers." He leaned in to Ray—and Ray quickly leaned back. "Lots of crazies out here, ya know."

Eric scoffed. "Tell me about it."

Skeeter looked confused. "About what?"

The old man rapped on the cab's rear window. "Hold on to 'em if ya got 'em, boys!"

Skeeter grabbed his balls and chuckled.

The engine revved and the pickup shot forward, kicking up a dust cloud. It accelerated down the dirt road and eventually disappeared around a thick band of trees.

ELEVEN

RAY AND ERIC SAT TRAPPED within the aluminum camper, its thick, stagnant air weighing heavily upon them. It was only a few minutes into their travel when ...

A long, wet fart escaped TC's ass. Bubbling out, the noise was amplified by the slick plastic of the wheelchair's seat.

"Ooops," Skeeter said, cupping a hand over his mouth out of embarrassment for his brother.

"Jesus. Christ," Eric said. "*Now* can we open the tailgate and free whatever just crawled out of his ass?"

Skeeter shook his head. "Sorry. No can do. He'll freak."

Pinching his nostrils shut, Eric wiped the beads of sweat sprouting across his brow and looked away. The air seemed nonexistent. Something, somewhere in the bed was rattling—metal against metal, like an incessant snare drum. Flies swarmed their heads, buzzing their ears and bouncing off their faces. One danced on Eric's eyelash, trying to taste the fluid coating his bloodshot eyeball. He swatted it away.

TC flinched and growled at the unexpected movement.

Ray avoided eye contact with Eric, knowing the simple act of ac-knowledging Eric's frustration might set his brother completely off. Then, to make matters worse ...

TC ripped loose more greasy flatulence.

Eric whimpered and quickly held his breath.

Skeeter's nose twitched like a rabbit. He licked his shoulder twice and sniffed again. "Cabbage?" he asked TC, who ignored him. "Smells like cabbage. We didn't eat cabbage last night! Who gave you cab—"

"Oh, for fuck's sake!" Eric screamed and lunged for the latch on the tailgate window to let in some air.

TC recoiled from the outburst.

"No! No!" Skeeter said. He bounced like an excited chimp and frantically licked his shoulder. "Keep it closed! Keep it closed! Don't upset TC!"

Ray grabbed Eric by his jacket collar and pulled him back, away from the window. "Calm down!"

"No, Ray! This is bullshit. This one over here," Eric pointed at TC, "is practically shittin' himself! And that one," he jabbed a finger at Skeeter, "with all that lick-lick-licking! What the hell is it that you're tasting?! Tell me! What?!"

Skeeter only shrugged and licked himself. TC broke his blank gaze, swinging his head in Ray and Eric's direction. A beat later, he singled out Eric and simply gave him the stink eye.

At his wit's end, Eric rose and went for the window again but Ray yanked him back down on his ass.

"Let go!" Eric said, shrugging off Ray's grasp. "I can't take this! I can't!"

"Just relax! I'm sure we're almost there."

During the commotion, Skeeter rose to his knees and stared out the small camper window over his shoulder. His hand opposite Ray and Eric dropped to the floor and felt around within the rumpled blankets.

"This will all be over soon," Ray told Eric. "And we'll be outside in the fresh air and it'll all be good again. Until then, just relax for me. Okay? Breathe. Just breathe."

Eric nodded. He took a few deep breaths and exhaled. It wasn't until he looked up and saw TC staring at him, drooling, that he threw in the towel. "Fuck it! I'm outta here!"

Skeeter gasped. "Ooh, potty mouth," he said without turning from his window.

Eric lunged for the tailgate again, his jacket and shirt tail riding up, exposing the guns in his rear waistband.

TC caught sight of them and cocked his head like a dog hearing a strange noise.

His back still to them, Skeeter continued staring out the window, his fingers roaming—searching—the blankets. Then his hand stopped on something hidden within the folds.

Ray clamped onto Eric's shoulder and threw him back against the bed wall. Enough was enough. If Eric accidentally fell out while trying to get the tailgate open, he could wind up like TC. "Sit the fuck back down!"

"Potty mouth!" Skeeter hollered over his shoulder—then licked it twice.

Eric shoved Ray back. "Get off me! I want out. I'd rather walk the rest of the way than put up with this freak show!"

As if on cue, Skeeter spun around, clapping wildly and throwing jazz hands in the air.

While TC reeled back, Ray and Eric sat dumbstruck over the eruption of energy.

"I'd rather walk," Skeeter sung while clapping, "In your light, Oh Lord ... "

TC's expression softened and became childlike over his brother's hymn. His eyes widened and a big old smile revealed gnarled, yellow buckteeth.

"Than crawl in your shadow, Oh Lord ..." Skeeter continued,

ignoring the fact he couldn't carry a tune worth a damn.

TC awkwardly clapped, trying, but failing miserably, to keep rhythm with Skeeter's song. Seeing his brother's validation, Skeeter pointed and winked at him. "I'd rather walk, Oh Lord ... walk right by your side!"

Ray and Eric exchanged glances over the den of insanity they'd somehow wandered into.

Skeeter's caterwauling grew louder and more intense. "Oh, Lord ... it's you ... yeah, you ... that I wanna follow into the light ...""

"Christ almighty!" Eric screamed. "Would you *shut up*!"

The blaspheme erased TC's smile, his jovial expression turned sour, and he glared at Eric.

Skeeter was too occupied with his powerful hymn to notice his guests' objection to his obnoxious singing.

"You two are fuckin' insane!" Eric said.

TC slowly raised his hand and pointed a beefy finger at Eric. Even wheelchair bound, the large man was still a formidable presence, probably clearing well over six feet in height if able to rise from the seat. Still pointing, another long, bubbling fart puttered from TC's ass. When it finally petered out, the large man glowed from such release.

Before Eric completely wigged out—and rightfully so—Ray snapped. "Okay! Ya know what? Maybe it's best you guys just let us out here."

"Thank God!" Eric said.

"Yes! Praise Jesus!" Skeeter said.

"Shut the fuck up!!" Eric screamed back, eyes bulging.

Skeeter finally fell silent. His hands stealthily lowered back to the blanket behind him.

Eric's gaze shifted from TC's thick finger (still pointing at him) over to Skeeter. "I'm tellin' you, *right* now. If your brother doesn't stop pointing at me, I'm gonna break off his fat finger and plug his ass with it so we don't have smell any more of his—"

MATT KURTZ

Skeeter sprung forward. A blade flashed. He slammed into Ray, pinning him against the wall with a straight razor pressed to his throat. The sudden attack sent Eric reeling back in the opposite direction.

TWELVE

PRESSING THE RAZOR AGAINST RAY'S jugular, Skeeter whipped around to Eric and roared, "You fuckin' move and I'll slit his throat!"

The old man behind the wheel spun and saw Skeeter taking control of the situation. He hooted and punched down on the gas. Yessiree, they'd caught a couple more for the fire.

Eric held up both hands to show he wasn't a threat. "No problem, Chief. Let's just be calm about this, okay? I'm sure we can work something out."

"You just sit there and shut your fuckin' mouth or I'll *bleed* him out!"

"Sure thing. No problem." Eric snuck a glance at TC to see if he, too, was in on the charade or simply the halfwit he appeared to be. Seeing the man sitting there, staring into space and drooling, Eric felt confident in the latter.

As the truck accelerated, its bad alignment and the uneven dirt road caused it to vibrate wildly. With every bump, the razor's polished blade danced across Ray's throat, scraping his whiskered neck and providing a shave he'd much rather do himself. Ray gritted his teeth and fought the shakes brought on by the adrenaline coursing through his system. In hindsight, he should've followed his gut before agreeing so quickly to hop in back. Should've just taken the truck as Eric intended from the get go. Or, at very least, paid way better attention to these two in back.

After two quick licks of his shoulder without ever taking his eyes off Ray, Skeeter yelled over at TC, "Hey, Buddy! You doing okay over there?"

TC gave no response—unless the drool stretching from his lower lip was code for something.

Skeeter studied Ray. "Wait until we get back to the house. Ya'll gonna loooove what's in store for ya!" He giggled and licked his lips. "You city boys are so damn trusting of us country fo—"

A gun cocked over Skeeter's shoulder. He whipped his head in its direction and was met by the business end of a .357 Taurus. The gun's muzzle pressed firmly against his temple.

"Not these city boys, shithead," Eric said. "Drop the razor and back away. Now!"

Skeeter grunted, a debate spinning through the hamster wheel behind his forehead. "Nuh-uh ... even if ya shoot, I can still slit his throat wide open."

"Highly doubt that, Chief. You might nick him. Draw a little blood. But when I squeeze this trigger, at point blank range, the muzzle velocity alone will knock you on your ass like you were just hit by a car."

"Bullshit," Skeeter said. "Nerves alone will let me—"

Eric pressed the muzzle harder against the young man's head. "I will kill you if you don't drop it. You have to the count of three. One ..."

Skeeter glared into Ray's eyes. The razor trembled in his hands. "Two ..."

A fresh wave of panic bubbled up in Ray. It was obvious Skeeter was bat-shit insane enough to try testing Eric's theory of whether he'd still be able to slit his throat after taking a bullet to the brain.

"Skeeter," Ray said, fighting like hell to sound calm. "He will kill you. Then your brother. Then Lew up front there. So just drop the razor and I promise no one will get hurt."

Skeeter slowly turned his head to look at TC, who sat drooling like the big oaf he was. Eric kept the barrel snug against the man's temple the entire time. Then Skeeter sighed, slowly removed the blade from Ray's throat, and dropped it.

The second the razor fell from Skeeter's grasp, Ray shoved him to the opposite side of the truck bed. He quickly rubbed his neck and was relieved to find his slick palm only covered with sweat.

Eric pulled out the second gun and offered Ray the deputy's revolver. "Here."

Ray glanced from Skeeter to TC and finally at the pistol. Then, to Eric's surprise, he snatched it up.

"Wanna tell shit-for-brains up there," Eric said, referencing Lew, "to pull over?"

The pounding at the back window drew the old man's attention off the road. Lew glanced over his shoulder and did a double take at Ray and Eric—both holding guns.

"Ah, shit," he said, grumbling over the sudden change of events.

"Pull over!" Ray screamed through the glass. "Now!"

The truck skidded to a stop along the two-lane dirt road bookended by a terrain of trees and overgrown brush. The camper window rose and the tailgate dropped. Ray leaped out and aimed his pistol back into the truck at TC and Skeeter as Eric slid up to the rear window and yelled at Lew through the glass.

"Take the keys out of the ignition and hold 'em out your window. And keep your other hand high on the steering wheel where we can see it!"

Once Lew did as he was told, Eric covered the two in the back while Ray strode to the cab to retrieve the keys. All this was accomplished without a single word spoken between Ray and Eric. They moved like a well-oiled machine and Eric couldn't help but smile over that fact.

Ray snatched the keys from the old man and shoved the gun in his face. "That was stupid. What? Were you plannin' on turning us in or something?"

Lew looked lost. "Turn ya in for what?"

Ray quickly brushed it off. There wasn't time for games. "Get out. Slowly. Hands high."

Lew hopped out and Ray patted him down, initially wincing over the man's damp clothes and the strong funk of body odor. Finding no weapons, Ray quickly wiped his hand on his pants leg and stepped back.

At the rear, Eric slid out of the bed. He grabbed the straight razor from the floor and hurled it into the field. "C'mon, Pooter," he told Skeeter. "Hop your ass out. Slowly."

Skeeter licked his shoulder and crawled out with hands held high. He let off a nervous giggle. "Look, I was just playin'. Ya know, all a joke. Ha ha. Right?"

"Yeah and I'm really fuckin' laughing." He motioned for Skeeter to move to the side of the truck. Once Skeeter was at a safe distance, Eric beckoned TC. "C'mon, Baby Huey. Roll your ass over here."

Skeeter stepped forward. "Don't you touch him."

Eric swung the gun, cocked its hammer, and plugged the barrel against Skeeter's forehead. "That's twice. There will not be a third time."

Ray came up behind his brother. "We got the keys. Let's go."

Eric uncocked the gun and pushed Skeeter back. "What about Baby Huey?" Eric said, hitching his thumb at the camper.

Ray was about to answer when movement in his periphery made

him whip his gun toward the front of the truck. "Hey!"

Lew froze in his tracks. Having been told to lean on the hood, he apparently decided to test the waters once left unattended and appeared one step away from making a mad dash into the neighboring brush.

"Where you think you're going there, Lew?"

The man sheepishly shrugged as both brothers aimed their guns at him.

Using the distraction, Skeeter snuck a glance at TC. He gave a quick nod to the hand buried between the big man's milky thighs.

This time, TC responded, nodding ever so slightly back.

"Get your ass over here," Ray told Lew.

"Yeah, sure. You got it." Lew joined them.

It was time to get going. Both Ray and Eric knew the longer they sat there the more vulnerable they became. Whatever the reason for the unsolicited attack, there could be more of these backwood pricks roaming the area, looking to do the same. Maybe it was sport out here in these parts because this wasn't about some citizen's arrest for assaulting the cop or a robbery for the wad of cash in Eric's pocket. These people apparently had their own nefarious agenda that went far beyond those things. And that was something Ray and Eric had zero interest in.

"You two," Eric told Lew and Skeeter, "get Double Stuffed out of the back."

Lew pointed at TC. "You see the size of that fucker? My back's shot to shit 'cause of the last time I tried to move his fat ass. Nuh-uh. I can't move him."

"Ya got him in there," Ray said.

Skeeter nodded. "By wheeling him up a wooden ramp."

"Yeah," Lew said. "The one we got back at the house."

Ray turned to Eric. "Fine. Let's get him out."

"Buuullshit. I ain't touching his stinky ass."

Ray sighed. "Then I'll do it myself. Take care of these two."

"Hold up. Got a better idea," Eric said. "How about we take his little wheelchair brake off, aim him toward the open tailgate, get in the truck, and just floor it. He'll fly right out. Problem solved."

Ray stared at Eric in disbelief, waiting for a sign he was only joking.

"C'mon." Eric reached for the keys. "I'll drive. You point him toward the road. And these two can catch him when he shoots out."

Ray pushed his hand away. "Just ... get these two out of my face."

"All rightey," Eric said to Lew and Skeeter. "You heard the man. Move your ass to the front of the truck."

As Eric led them away, Ray shoved the gun in his waistband and climbed into the truck bed, mindful not to make any sudden moves.

"Lay down," Eric said. "Right there."

Both looked at where he was pointing. "You want us to lie in the middle of the road?" Lew asked.

"Has any traffic come by this entire time?" Eric said.

"No. But still. The middle of the—"

Eric cocked the gun. "Your chances of getting run over out here are a hell of a lot less likely than me just shooting your ass. Now do it!"

"Fine. Fine," Lew said. "You win." He and Skeeter walked to the middle of the dirt road and dropped to their bellies.

Ray knelt before TC and assessed the situation. What was the best way to get the big guy out without upsetting him? Just take things slow, right?

With one arm still dangling at his side and the other buried deep in his crotch, TC stared off into space. Before doing anything, Ray gave the wheelchair the once over to figure out its mechanics. A lever on each wheel released the brakes. A skirt hung about six inches below the seat, probably to discreetly hold a bedpan or colostomy bag. Other than that, there wasn't much more to it.

Okay. Here goes nothing.

On all fours, he released both brakes and carefully reached between TC's calves and grabbed hold of a horizontal bar running just beneath the curtain. Slowly shuffling back on his knees, he moved to the open tailgate then pulled on the chair to roll it toward him.

It didn't budge.

Was there some third brake he failed to notice? He pulled again but it still didn't move. Maybe something was wedged under a wheel. Crawling forward, Ray brushed aside the blankets for a better look.

What he discovered made no sense.

The wheels were bolted to the truck bed.

So how the hell did they wheel him——?

Then it quickly dawned on Ray this was another ploy. His first instinct was to look up at TC for confirmation.

The man was smiling down at Ray with a devilish grin.

In the blink of an eye, TC withdrew the hand hidden between his thighs. It brandished a sawed-off, double barrel shotgun with pistol grip. The gun was modified enough to easily fit within the hole cut in his seat—the ruffled skirt hanging below helped conceal the weapon.

Ray went for his pistol, but TC was quicker, slamming the shotgun into Ray's temple. The blow sent him pinwheeling back. He tumbled to the floor, the revolver falling out of his waistband.

Springing from the wheelchair, TC kicked the gun out of Ray's reach and leaped on him like an angry gorilla.

THIRTEEN

THE TRUCK VIOLENTLY ROCKED. ITS shocks groaned under the weight of the struggle taking place within.

Eric spun around just as the vehicle creaked to a stop.

Inside, TC overpowered Ray from behind with a single-arm chokehold and shoved the double barrel into the man's temple. Dragging his prey, TC scooted deeper into the truck until his shoulders were flush with the rear wall of the cab. It was the best position for cover given their location, keeping them low enough to remain out of sight through both the cab and camper windows. That just left the open tailgate, which was why he was using Ray as a shield.

Ray fought for air as the chokehold tightened, clawing at the large arm in an attempt to pry it loose. With eyes bulging and face growing purple, he gasped for a breath that refused to enter. TC took the gun off Ray and aimed it at the open tailgate. He waited for Eric to enter the kill zone.

Seconds ticked by. Eric did not appear.

TC swung his bald noggin left and right, dribbling on Ray's head. He searched for Eric in the surrounding windows but, from his low angle, only the bright blue Texas sky was visible. He grunted and scooted closer for a better look, pulling Ray with him. Craning his thick neck, TC peeked out the nearest window and spotted Lew and Skeeter lying on their bellies, spread-eagle in the middle of the road with only their heads raised. They stared back at him, wide-eyed. Fearful. It appeared their final element of surprise had run its course.

He searched back and forth, up and down the road, desperate to locate Eric.

Grunting, he whirled around to check the window behind him.

And Eric stood there waiting, his pistol pressed against it and sighted on TC's oversized melon.

TC gasped. Then swung the sawed-off at Eric. Before the large brute could take aim, Eric dropped the hammer on his revolver.

Ray winced from the explosion and squeezed his eyes shut. The plexiglass window blew inward then a portion of TC's skull evaporated. A warm, pink spray splattered the opposite wall and misted the air.

TC's grip loosened and his body slumped over. Ray broke free and slid out from under the man's grasp and tumbled from the truck, landing on the hard, dirt road. He gasped for a breath to fill his aching lungs. His trembling hands wiped at the blood and brains coating his face.

Eric flew to his brother's side. He knelt beside Ray, but kept his gun trained on the truck bed. "Are you okay?"

There was a thunderous explosion and a section of the camper's roof blew apart.

Eric pushed Ray down then dropped for cover himself.

Barely able to catch his breath, Ray was still stuck in flight mode. He belly-crawled for cover within the weeds beside the road, his bulging eyes rattling in their sockets.

Eric sprung up and made a move for the truck bed.

Inside, TC lay convulsing. Both barrels of his shotgun were

smoking while its tip rattled a macabre Morse code against the metal liner. A portion of the roof was blown out, the jagged aluminum pulled upward like gnarled fingers clawing for the sky. Surrounding the larger opening were dozens of smaller holes from the wide pellet spray. It was only a death twitch that happened to squeeze off both barrels of the sawed-off. But the shots were wild. And the gun was now empty. There was no threat.

Eric stared with grim fascination at the large hole exposing part of TC's skull and what looked like raw hamburger hanging out. His stomach twisted at the sight. He quickly reached in and pried the small shotgun out of the man's grasp to end its nerve-shattering rapping. Once the gun was removed, TC went still.

The man was dead.

Eric ran back to Ray and helped him up out of the weeds. "You okay?" He looked at his brother's gore-soaked face. "That's just his blood, right?"

Ray nodded and wiped at the blood using the back of his hands.

"Are you hurt?"

He shook his head and quickly stripped down to his pocket tee then balled up the blood-spattered button down and used it as a rag to clean himself.

"Okay. Stay here." Eric rushed to the front of the truck.

Ray threw aside the soiled shirt and rubbed his throat. His airway felt like a crimped garden hose. But with each breath, it inched open, allowing more air to enter. The ringing in his ears, either from lack of blood flow to his brain or such close proximity to the gunshot, was also slowly subsiding.

"Oh, shit!" Eric said. "We've got problems." He bolted past Ray to check the opposite side of the road.

Ray tried to ask "What?" but it only came out a croak.

"Those two shitheads!" Eric said. "They're gone! Took off during the commotion." He continued searching for them.

Ray shambled back to the truck and stared into the open tailgate.

Blood was splashed across one side of the interior like the canvas of a Pollock painting. The sunlight spilling through the large hole made by the shotgun blast cast a spotlight upon the large corpse lying belly up inside.

Ray groaned and forced himself to look at TC's corpse. Being reunited with Eric, is this what the future had in store for him? He stared at the body in silence until gravity took hold of a piece of brain stuck to the wall, making it peel off and land with a wet splat. Turning away, he spotted his revolver peeking out from under a blanket. He grabbed it with a trembling hand and wiped off its blood-spattered surface.

Eric popped up behind his brother. "I don't see 'em anywhere."

Ray jumped and almost dropped the gun.

"They can't be far," Eric continued, "but we gotta get out of here. Now."

Ray gave no response. His gaze shifted from his own blood-caked hands to TC's corpse.

"Hey. You listening?"

Nothing.

"Dammit, Ray! They could be getting help. We have to move!"

Ray nodded slightly, then something clicked and his daze broke.

That something was the need for survival.

"Okay ... Okay." He fished the keys from his pocket and tossed them to Eric. "Start the truck. I'll find a spot to dump the body."

Eric hopped in the pickup and fired it up. The overwhelming stench coming from the burlap sacks covering the passenger seat nearly made him gag. Whatever their contents, they were all about to be dumped on the side of the road along with TC's body. He slammed the gearshift into reverse and peered out the back window, waiting further instructions from his brother.

Ray sprinted to the far side of the road. Another ravine ran parallel to their path. It was nothing compared to the one they crashed the Galaxie into, but definitely deep enough to conceal a body from any passerby. Ray whistled and waved the truck over. The vehicle charged backwards and skidded to a stop, parking perpendicular to the road with its tailgate aimed at the edge of the embankment. Eric killed the engine, hopped out, and joined Ray.

"I'll take care of him," Ray said, referring to TC. "You wipe down the walls. Especially the windows. If we're gonna drive this thing, it can't look like some mobile slaughterhouse."

Eric seemed thrilled over the sudden shift in Ray's demeanor. The man was finally taking charge again, quite a welcome return compared to the pathetic drunk from last night. His enthusiasm didn't go unnoticed.

"I'm just trying to unfuck this situation," Ray said. "Before it gets worse. That's all. Now move."

That was good enough for Eric. He grabbed a blanket and got to work on the camper windows.

Ray spread out a comforter the best he could within the cramped quarters and rolled TC's body onto it. He hopped out, grabbed both corners of the blanket, and pulled the corpse closer to the tailgate.

Eric wiped at one of the gore-covered windows. The first pass smeared blood across its surface. The next wipe cleared enough of it for him to see out of and spot the approaching vehicle about a quarter mile down the road.

"Shit," Eric said. "We got company!"

FOURTEEN

A BLACK PICKUP HEADED TOWARD THEM, cruising at a casual pace. Still, within seconds it'd be close enough its driver might be able to make out the corpse's bloody legs dangling off the tailgate.

Ray glanced at TC then spun around to size up the ravine. *Dump him in quick,* his mind screamed, *before the driver can make out it's a body.*

No. Even if they think it's only trash, it'll draw suspicion ... and probably anger because of the whole Don't Mess With Texas mantra about littering. Ray snuck a peek at the black pickup closing the gap between them. He had to act fast. "Get him back in and cover him up." Eric pulled and Ray pushed until TC was concealed in the truck. "I'll handle this. Finish getting the blood off the window. Now!"

Eric nodded and wiped faster.

"If they stop, let me handle it," Ray said. "Even if it all goes to hell, let me handle it. Got it?"

"Sure thing. But, if anyone else screws with us—"

"I'll handle it. Just stay here. Stay out of sight." Ray slammed the tailgate shut and lowered the camper window.

Eric threw his hand up and stopped it. "Don't close me in here. Leave it open so I can breathe."

"If it's left open, and they wind up stopping, they might be tempted to take a peek inside. Just tough it out for a minute. You'll be okay." Ray sealed his brother in without further debate.

Now for a plan. Concealing himself on the opposite side of the orange truck, Ray paced and racked his electrified brain for a believable scenario. *Okay, you're on the side of the road. Why?*

A flat.

He looked at the fully inflated tires beside him and knew it wouldn't work.

Back to the slowly advancing truck … now a few yards away. Any moment it'd roll past and spot him on the other side.

Dead battery? No. If they stopped to ask, they'll offer a jump. Needs to be something minor. Something that wouldn't need any assistance so they'll just be on their way.

The growl of the black truck's engine grew louder.

Ray ran to the back tire to put as much distance between him and the newcomer as possible—especially if things went south and he was forced to duck behind the truck for cover. He shoved the pistol into his rear waistband and covered it with his shirt. Squatting to still remain mobile, he faced the approaching truck then reached over the top of the rear tire and acted like he was messing with something there.

In the bed, Eric crouched out of sight and replaced the spent casing of the bullet used on TC. With the flick of his wrist, he snapped the cylinder back into place and put his thumb on the hammer. Ready for action.

The hefty chug of the approaching vehicle's engine vibrated the orange truck's body.

Ray took a deep breath. Showtime. If asked, he'd say he ran over a piece of wire or rope that snared around the rear axle. He started his performance, writhing the arm buried deep in the tire well as if trying to work an imaginary cord loose from behind the wheel.

The front of the black pickup appeared at the corner of the parked truck. It crawled forward, crunching over the graveled road.

Ray slid his eyes in its direction and stared at the 1987 Chevy Silverado with chrome running boards and six-inch lifts. Its pristine paint job was like an ebony mirror reflecting the distorted image of the orange pickup. The Silverado's dark tint failed to reveal even the slightest outline of the driver or any passengers within.

Since failure to acknowledge the passerby might raise suspicion, Ray gave the vehicle a nod and friendly smile then returned his attention to the rear tire while constantly repositioning himself to never lose sight of the Silverado.

Eric carefully rose and peeked out a camper window.

The black pickup slowly passed.

"That-a-girl," Eric whispered. "Keep your ass moving."

The truck gradually accelerated down the road until becoming a dot on the horizon.

Once it disappeared, Ray rose and met Eric at the tailgate.

"Caught us a break, huh?" Eric said, lifting the window.

"I don't like it."

Eric dropped the tailgate and pushed his way out of the truck. "What? What's the problem?"

"Out here, people stop to help ya if you're broken down. Or at least throw out an offer to."

"Maybe they don't believe in southern hospitality."

Ray kept glancing back at the horizon. "They also know what their neighbors drive. A truck like this orange piece of shit is too unique. We should've just ducked out of sight. Made it look abandoned." He shook his head. "That driver knew. He knew."

"What's done is done," Eric said. "Now, it's best we lighten our load and get the hell outta here before we get any more visitors."

TC's body was concealed under a thin layer of brush at the bottom of the ravine. Once the corpse was hidden, Ray climbed into the driver's seat … and winced at the cabin's god-awful stench. Eric stood at the open passenger door and fanned the air.

"I know," he said, nodding at the numerous lumpy sacks that took up his side of the cab. "Nasty ol' fucker must have been out collecting roadkill for dinner."

While Eric began tossing the bags from the truck, Ray fired up the engine and white-knuckled the steering wheel and did a double take at his left hand. There was a red ribbon across his wedding band. It was TC's dried blood. A whimper escaped his lips. Eric paused and watched his brother scrub the ring clean using the end of his untucked shirt.

His attention on Ray, Eric yanked at a bag snared on something under the seat. The sack ripped and a large, hairy mass fell out, landing on the passenger floorboard with a dull thud. "Oh, shit!" he said and jumped away from the dead animal.

Ray leaned over and stared into the footwell. Whatever it was, it was a balled mess of blood-matted hair. Then he noticed a pale, fleshy nub poking out from the tangled mop.

The nub had a gold loop through it. An earring. It was no animal.

Ray lurched back from the severed head and slammed against the driver's door.

The brothers locked eyes, each waiting for the other to offer up an explanation. Eric glanced at the shovel near his feet and remembered their first glimpse of the old man. "Ray …? Was that sick old fuck burying them in that field? Or digging them up?"

It took a few moments for Ray to find his voice. "Is one better than the other?"

Both stared at all the bags of body parts littering the road around Eric's feet. He kicked away a few that seemed to be creeping back toward him.

Moments later, he used the shovel to scoop the woman's severed head out of the truck. When it hit the ground with a hollow thump like a dropped coconut, both men shuddered at the sound.

Once the passenger side was cleared, Eric brushed the seat with his jacket sleeve then climbed in and slammed the door shut.

The orange truck revved its engine, coughed up a toxic cloud of exhaust, then lunged forward and accelerated down the dirt road, leaving behind the remains of unspeakable horrors ... as its driver and passenger unknowingly sped toward all new ones.

FIFTEEN

BARRELING DOWN THE NARROW FARM road, the black Chevy Silverado approached a small thicket of trees. As the pickup drew closer, two figures ran out from behind the foliage and waved the vehicle down.

Once the truck came to a stop, Skeeter and Lew shuffled over to the beefy red-haired man wedged behind the wheel.

"What the hell is going on?" Red, the driver, asked.

"We got problems," Lew said.

"No shit. I realized that a few miles back when I saw your truck there without you in it. What happened?" Red looked around. "And where's TC?"

"They killed him," Skeeter said.

Lew added, "Dumb sumbitch got himself shot."

Skeeter raised a fist to his temple then flicked his fingers out, pantomiming the explosive exit wound of a headshot. Without missing a beat, he licked his shoulder twice and smiled.

Only Red seemed disturbed over TC's demise. He white-knuckled the steering wheel, making it creak under his vice-like grip.

"And now they's trying to get away," Skeeter said. "Back to the highway."

Red shook his head. "They ain't goin' nowhere. Get in."

"Who the fuck are these people?" Eric asked over the engine's rattle.

"All I wanna know is how we get our asses back to the highway."

Eric shook his head. "Are we even heading the right way?"

Both men scanned the surrounding fields then looked at the wooded area ahead.

"This is the direction the old bastard was driving," Ray answered.

"And you *really* think he was taking us back to the highway?"

"I don't know. But figure it's best to go polar opposite of that black truck, especially if he was on to us."

It sounded like a plan to Eric. And having Ray back in the driver's seat—both figuratively and literally—sure felt good.

The orange truck blew into the wooded area so fast its occupants never caught sight of the dirt trail running perpendicular to the main road. By the time its dust cleared the intersection, a large black shape materialized out of the haze.

The Silverado sat recessed in the trail. The truck's engine growled, then the black and chrome beast crept forward onto the main road, preparing to give chase.

Shrugging off his jacket from the rising temperature, Eric emptied its pockets, removing first the sealed envelope—Ray's birthday gift—and then the box of bullets. He placed the envelope on the open seat between them and began fiddling with the ammo.

Ray glanced down at the envelope. The air rushing in through the windows caused the paper to dance across the seat. Before it got sucked outside, Ray slammed his hand on top of it. Appreciating the save, Eric took the envelope and tucked it under his leg then emptied the half box of bullets and gave Ray his share. Both men stuffed the brass into their front pockets.

A long moment of silence passed between them. Ray fidgeted, tapping the wheel. Then, he had to ask, "How sure are you it's him?"

When Eric appeared lost, Ray glanced down at the envelope for clarification.

"Trust me," Eric said. "It's him." He folded the envelope and stuck it in his back pocket.

"What if you're wrong?"

"I'm not."

"Yeah, but what if—"

"I'm not."

"We thought the same thing about Jacobs, remember?"

Eric wanted to spare Ray the gory details, but if he was going to keep pushing …

"He cuts off their finger," he said. "The index finger. It's his calling card."

The jarring memory of his broken Rachel reaching up to him with her mutilated hand caused a hissing intake of breath. Avoiding eye contact with his brother, Ray gripped the wheel tight and only nodded.

Eric continued, "He saves them as trophies. Mementos." He shook his head. "Sick fuck."

Instinctively, Ray rubbed his chest, his fingers clawing at his shirt, searching for the small piece of solace that hung around his neck. He found it and gripped the ring tight.

Eric stared out the passenger window. "Ya know, whether I go at this solo or not, killing this son-of-a-bitch is gonna force me to go off the grid. On a permanent vacation. Where no one will find me." He turned back to Ray. "And when I do, I want you to come with me. 'Cause I miss ya, man. I miss my big bro. We're the only family we got left."

Ray glanced at his younger brother. They locked eyes for a moment and Eric waited with bated breath for a sign the feeling was mutual. After a long beat, Ray nodded then turned back to the road. The simple gesture was enough acknowledgement for Eric to have hope again, something that was missing at the bar last night.

It was definitely a first step in the right direction.

"Who is this guy you'll have to go into hiding for?" Ray asked.

"He's just a hired gun for various jobs. Killing him isn't gonna bring much heat. But the money I skimmed in order to pay off the people that led me to him ... now *that* put me on the radar of some top-tier people. And that's why I gotta get lost for a very long time."

"Skimmed? Who?"

"LaMorte."

Ray tried to speak. But only exhaled.

"I know," Eric said. He looked away, back out the window. "I did a couple jobs for him and took what I needed before he realized what was missing."

"How much?"

"Enough for him to send out a crew to get it back. So, besides the obvious ... that's the *other* reason why I want you in Oklahoma. To watch my back."

Ray groaned. "This just keeps getting better and better. Anything else you wanna fill me in on? Things I should know that might affect—"

An explosion outside the driver's window sent a swarm of angry hornets buzzing by Ray's head. The shotgun pellets blew apart his door mirror, evaporating it into the air stream behind them. Stray pellets shattered the windshield and sent cracks rippling through its surface like an ice skin breaking over a frozen pond.

Ray gasped and stomped the brake pedal. The black Silverado rocketed past them, but not before getting off another shot from its open passenger window. Because of Ray's quick reaction, the second shot sprayed over the orange truck's hood and completely missed them.

Red and the shotgun-toting Lew, with Skeeter wedged between them, all spun around and saw the orange truck skidding to a stop.

"Goddammit!" Lew yelled.

"Think ya got 'em!" Skeeter said. All riled up, he triple licked his shoulder.

"Bullshit!" Lew racked the shotgun. The spent shell ejected, bounced off the windshield, and came to a rolling stop on the dashboard. "Didn't get shit with your monkey ass jumping around! Ya kept bumping me and threw off my aim, dipshit!"

"Told ya he shouldn't be up here!" Red scooped the smoking shell off the dash and quickly wiped at its shiny, Armor All-ed surface to make sure it was blemish free. "Should be riding in the back instead like the dog he is."

Skeeter frowned over the lack of respect.

Red didn't give two shits about his hurt feelings. "Hang on for round two, boys!" he said, rolling the steering wheel.

Through their cracked windshield, Ray and Eric watched the Silverado make a U-turn for another attack.

"You okay?" Ray said.

Eric nodded and pulled out his gun. Ray did the same then wiped his brow, making sure it was sweat and not blood trickling down his face. He scanned the perimeter for a way out, saw a possibility, and looked back at the approaching truck.

Eric leaned out his window to take a shot when Ray pulled him back inside.

"No! Just ... hang on!" Ray stomped the gas. The truck shuddered, but accelerated, and for being such a piece-a-shit, quickly picked up speed.

The old orange vehicle barreled toward the shiny black one in a deadly game of chicken.

"Get these fuckers!" Lew said.

Red punched the accelerator and gripped the wheel tight at three and nine. His heart was nearly thumping out of his chest. Those two sons-of-bitches responsible for killing TC needed to pay but was he really willing to total his truck over it? If the two vehicles collided at sixty-plus miles per hour, they'd *all* die. Now where was the logic in that? He hissed and secretly slid his foot to the edge of the gas pedal, closer to the brake.

Preparing for a possible collision, Skeeter licked himself and dug deeper into the seat for his safety belt.

Eric glanced at the oncoming truck. "What's your plan, Ray? Tell me you're not stupid enough to play chicken with these idiots!"

No response. Ray kept on the gas, his attention locked on the road ahead.

"Screw this!" Eric made another attempt to lean out and fire but Ray stopped him again.

"Just trust me!" Ray pointed up ahead. To the right. "There! Look!"

Eric saw it and glanced back at the truck racing at them. "Then make it quick, man!"

Ray mashed the accelerator, making the engine scream.

The two trucks sped toward each other, the hundred-yard distance between them collapsing with every passing millisecond.

"They ain't backin' down!" Red yelled. "And I ain't wreckin' my truck over this shit!"

The old man leaned over and clamped his hand on the steering wheel to prevent Red from swerving. "You do it, ya goddamn coward!"

"C'mon, Ray! C'mon!" Eric pounded the dashboard. "Move it!"

Ray stood on the gas until the pedal was flush with the floor.

Eric instinctively braced for impact, but knew damn well if they collided they'd be ejected through the windshield. "Do it, man! Do it!!"

Once close enough to glimpse the three faces materializing behind the opposite windshield—most notably the ginger-haired, bug-eyed driver that was screaming wildly—Ray jerked the wheel to the right.

Both trucks roared past one another, inches apart, and rocked from the colliding wind streams.

Red gasped and hit the brakes. "Oh, Sweet Jesus! Thank you!"

Behind them, the orange truck fishtailed in the dirt, kicking up a wave of earth, and quickly regained its course along the single-lane trail running perpendicular to the main road.

Lew stared out the back window and watched his stolen truck disappear into the woods. He reached across Skeeter and slapped at Red. "They're getting away! Turn around! Turn around, godammit!"

Red nodded and spun the wheel. "Aight then."

SIXTEEN

HIS HAIR FLAPPING WILDLY, ERIC hung out the window and waited for their pursuers to appear in the billowing dust cloud behind them.

The road ahead narrowed, its foliage squeezing tighter.

Ray kept the vehicle to the left so Eric's head wouldn't get ripped off by an overextended tree limb. Because of that, the branches clawed at the driver's side, raking long gouges into the paint. Eric heard the scraping and jumped back in then Ray maneuvered the truck back to the center of the narrow trail.

"We lose 'em?" Ray said, checking the rearview.

Eric studied his side mirror. "Don't know." It was near impossible to make out anything in the tiny reflection from all the shaking and vibrating caused by the bumpy road.

Then ... a flash of chrome came from somewhere in the trees behind them.

"Shit!" Eric said and spun to the rear window.

"I know. I know. I see it!" Ray whipped around another bend. Up ahead, the thick foliage bottlenecked their path but the orange truck charged forward and shot out of the strangling vegetation and into the open area beyond.

The landscape ahead changed considerably, their path now bisecting a large hill with both sides of its surface littered with large rocks and trees.

Ray attempted to take in the area for the best escape route, but the overwhelming adrenaline rush destroyed his concentration. Turn left? Go straight? Turn right? The truck felt like it was vibrating out of his hands. The engine roar was deafening. His leg began to cramp from standing on the gas pedal. Stinging sweat rolled into his eyes. His brain felt on fire. He needed a quick reset from the sensory overload.

He slammed the brakes and let the truck skid to a stop.

Eric lurched forward and bounced off the dash. He stared at Ray as if the man had just sprouted a third eye. "What're you doing? They're right behind us. Go!"

His eyes shifting back and forth, Ray nodded, but not in response to Eric's command. "Okay. Okay. I got a plan."

The black truck glided around a narrow turn. Red tapped the brakes and swerved to avoid the overhanging branch.

"Would you speed up!" Lew said.

"He don't wanna scratch his truck none," Skeeter said.

"Damn straight!" Red answered, carefully maneuvering through the bottleneck. "Besides, ya both know there's only one place this road—" He stood on the brake. "Oh, shit!"

"What?!" Skeeter said. He'd been looking at Red when the man's eyes went wide over something ahead. By the time he swung back to the road, the cloud of dust from the truck skidding to a stop blew forward and completely enveloped their vehicle like a blinding sandstorm. He licked his shoulder and waited as it slowly lifted.

About fifty yards away, just between the tree shrouded hills, the orange truck faced them with engine idling.

Skeeter, Lew, and Red watched the vehicle in silence.

"What're they doing?" Red whispered.

Lew shrugged. "Bastards wanna play chicken again, huh?"

"Yeah," Skeeter said. "Floor it!"

"Fuck that hell," Red said. "Told ya, I ain't wrecking my truck!" He squinted, trying to see past the sun glaring off the opposite vehicle's cracked windshield.

The orange truck's tailpipe coughed puffs of exhaust. The vehicle was definitely running—idling, ready for action—but its former occupants weren't inside. They were high up on the mount, flanking the pickup.

Ray peeked out from behind a thick tree trunk and spied Eric on the opposite hill, crouched behind a rock with gun drawn.

Eric ticked his head at the black truck down the road. *Let's move.*

Ray shook him off and held up a finger. *Be patient.*

Both men turned back to the Silverado, waiting for it to roll forward. Into their kill zone.

"C'mon. Move your asses a little closer," Eric said. The truck was too far away to get a clean shot. Unless he and Ray moved in, they'd be wasting ammo.

The black Silverado sat frozen.

Eric glanced back to Ray who was already staring at him. Ray shrugged, unsure why the truck wasn't moving any closer. Had they been spotted? Eric motioned that they rush it. Be the aggressor.

Ray knew he was right. Every passing second meant they were losing the element of surprise. The truck could slam in reverse and go fetch reinforcements and then they'd really be screwed. But a small part of him wished for that to happen because their leaving could give Eric and him enough of a head start to reach the highway before they even made it back and avoid any more unnecessary bloodshed.

But killing TC had already stirred that hornet's nest. There was no way this could end peacefully. It was about self-preservation now. These people wanted to kill them both and were willing to die trying. He was knee deep in this shit without the possibility of refusal unlike Eric's offer regarding Oklahoma.

Them or us, Ray thought, psyching himself up for what needed to be done. *Them or us*. He gritted his teeth and exhaled.

Them. Or us.

Ray raised his gun and nodded at Eric. *Let's roll.*

Using the trees and brush for cover, the brothers slowly made their way closer to the Silverado. Once within range, they could rain fire upon its occupants from above and finally end this madness.

"Don't like this," Lew said, glaring at his orange truck.

Red reached under his seat and pulled out a revolver. Pushing open its cylinder, he checked to make sure it was still loaded—that those idgets TC and Skeeter hadn't been playing with it again, leaving it with nothing but empty casings. Confirming the live ammo, he snapped the cylinder back into place. Time to get down to business. Lew had his shotgun. He had a pistol. And Skeeter had ... "Where's your gun, dipshit?"

Skeeter shrugged and licked his shoulder. "Back with TC. He wanted to use it this time."

Lew scoffed. "Lot of fucking good it did his dumb ass."

"Hey!" Red said. "Show a little fuckin' respect!"

Lew sighed.

Red addressed Skeeter, "Well, ya can't go into this holding only your pecker." He pointed at the glove box. "Ya left one of your lil' pig stickers in here last time. Go on. Get it, so ya got something at least."

Skeeter pulled open the compartment and found one of his straight razors inside. It wasn't his favorite, but it'd do. He flipped it open and saw what looked like rust coating its polished blade. No, not rust ... dried blood. His lower lip quivered with excitement.

Using the blade was so much more personal than any gun. There was nothing better than watching someone's reaction as the blade slices—

"Hey, stupid!" Red said. "We're talkin' to you!"

Skeeter glanced up from the blade to find Red and the old man staring at him.

"You ready or not?" Lew asked.

Skeeter nodded.

Red turned back to the road ahead. "Aight then. Let's do this." He shifted his foot from brake to gas and slowly pressed down.

Up ahead, Eric took the lead with Ray following on the opposite side. Both were closing the distance, fast. They planned to step out onto the landing, aim down at the road, and empty their weapons diagonally into the truck's roof. The bullets would pierce the cab from both sides, crisscrossing for maximum coverage. Both men picked up the pace to reach the truck faster.

Lew screamed, "Wait!" and threw a hand up.

Red hit the brakes. "What is it?"

The old man's eyes darted between the orange truck and the surrounding high ground. "It's a set up! They ain't in the truck! Get us outta here!"

The reverse lights lit up on the Silverado. Its tires spun in the dirt before catching traction. The pickup lurched backwards and raced for cover back within the narrow opening of the densely wooded area.

Eric saw them retreating and broke into a full on charge.

Shots erupted from both sides of the Silverado.

In response, Ray ducked for cover behind a tree. Eric held his advance, carelessly stepping out onto the open crest and firing down at the vehicle. Before he could take more precise aim, the truck rocketed backwards under a low hanging canopy of tree branches and disappeared from Eric's hilltop view. He leaped over the landing and slid down the embankment to get a clean shot. Running out into the middle of the road, he drew a bead on the truck and squeezed off three shots before the rolling dust cloud—kicked up by its spinning tires—devoured the pickup from sight.

Ray slid up to his brother and fired blindly into the wall of dust.

The shifting breeze caught the cloud and blew it in their direction. Hot, blinding grit blasted their faces, making them turn away. When it finally passed, the black Silverado was gone, retreating the way it came.

The brothers stood frozen, their ears ringing from gunfire. Eric kept his pistol trained on the foliage, hoping to spot the truck somewhere within.

But there was nothing.

Ray lowered his gun. "C'mon. Before they bring others." He started back to the orange pickup.

Eric scanned the trees at the narrow opening one last time then turned and followed Ray.

Both men stopped in front of the idling truck to reload.

"What now?" Eric asked.

"We hop in and drive like hell outta here." He nodded behind the old pickup. "That way."

"You sure?"

"Well, backtracking is suicidal," Ray continued. "We could be driving right into an ambush. Nuh-uh. We follow this road and hope it leads to the highway. Or some gas station we can stop at and ask directions."

"Shit, we pull up at some gas station in this thing and ..." He shook his head. "Like you said, they all know what their neighbors drive. We'll probably be shot on sight."

"We'll cross that bridge when we get to it. Until then, we got a truck that runs and practically has a full tank of gas. So we hop in, and drive like a bat outta h—"

The steady idle under the hood quickly transformed into something that sounded like a cat coughing up a hairball. Then the engine sputtered and died, its creaking fan snapping to a halt.

Both men stared at the truck in disbelief.

"Oh, you gotta be fuckin' kidding," Ray said.

SEVENTEEN

WITH GUN DRAWN, ERIC STOOD outside the driver's door and kept watch while Ray fiddled under the hood, trying his damndest to resurrect the engine.

Fifteen minutes had passed, an eternity to be stranded out in the open. Eric grew nervous standing guard. The hair prickling on his neck told him they were being watched. He knew those inbreds were out there. Somewhere. Just waiting.

Ray pulled a grease-coated hand out of the engine. "Try her now."

Eric hopped in and turned the key. The engine clicked twice, then ... nothing.

Ray pushed away from the vehicle. "Dammit. This is freakin' useless without tools." He wiped his hands on a ratty towel taken from the camper.

Eric snatched his jacket off the seat and removed the compact binoculars from it, transferring the lenses from coat to shirt pocket. "Then we move on."

"Where?"

"Anywhere but here." He threw his jacket back into the truck to get rid of the dead weight. "Clock's ticking, remember?"

Ray nodded. "Then we see where the road leads."

"Fine by me. Let's go." Eric kicked the driver's door shut, leaving behind a size-eleven dent in the shape of his boot.

"Whaddaya think they're saying?" Skeeter asked Lew and Red.

All three hid behind a large log lying in the dense overgrowth about seventy-five yards away.

"If I was close enough to hear 'em, stupid," Lew said, his anger simmering, "I'd be close enough to shoot 'em. Now wouldn't I?"

Skeeter had to think it over, which pissed Lew off even more. Now was not the time to be pushing the old man's buttons.

Staring off into the distance, Red fished a leathery, drawstring tobacco pouch from his pocket. "Look. They's on the move."

All three watched as Ray and Eric abandoned the truck and headed down the stretch of road behind it.

"Wanna get after 'em now?" Red asked. He shoved a wad of chew in his mouth.

"Nah. Let 'em wander a bit. Let down their guard. Think they lost us. Besides, only one thing up that road to welcome 'em."

Skeeter grew squirrelly with excitement. "I think we should go get 'em. They already slipped us once. So who's to say they won't—"

Lew held up his index finger. A final warning to the young man.

"All I know," Red said, "is I want the sack of the one that offed TC." He raised his tobacco pouch. Tiny pubic hairs covered its flaking surface. "Need me another pouch. This one's about had it."

"Fine by me," Lew said. "As long as I get its contents when ya empty it. Got special plans for them stones."

Red wiggled his brows and smiled. "Aight then."

"Then what about the other one?" Skeeter said. "I think it's time I got one all to myself. Been thinkin' of some new ways to—"

The old man blew a gasket. He snatched a tree limb off the

ground, one roughly the size of a baseball bat, and rammed it into Skeeter's stomach, folding him over in pain.

Red watched the assault and simply snickered.

In a hissing whisper, Lew said, "We're in this mess because you couldn't handle them in the first place!" He raised the branch over his head. "And *now* you think you're man enough to have one all for yourself?"

Lew slammed the branch across Skeeter's back, crumpling him to his knees. Skeeter covered his head and squealed as the old man pummeled him with repeated strikes from the makeshift club.

"You get nothing! Nothing! Until Precious does!"

The final blow snapped the branch over Skeeter's back, collapsing him into a fetal position. Lew tossed the broken branch aside, took a deep breath, and hooted. "That's it! Now I'm all riled up. Let's hunt!" He strode over to the thicket of trees concealing the Silverado pickup.

Red approached Skeeter and waited for the young man to lower his arms and look up. When he did, Red spit a nasty stream of tobacco juice onto Skeeter's face.

The warm, brown fluid got in his eyes and mouth, eliciting a squeal like a stuck piglet.

Red kicked him in the gut to shut him up. "Ya heard him, shit-fer-brains. Get your ass movin'."

Skeeter wiped away the mixture of Red's spit and his own tears covering his face then scrambled to his feet. Half blinded, skin flushed, he placed his back to the two men walking away and shoved a hand down his pants to adjust his erection caused by the beating. He quickly pinned his pecker up into his waistband and stretched his t-shirt down to cover it. Carefully waddling over to the Silverado, he hoped they wouldn't notice the evidence of his arousal. After all, the last thing he needed was to be castrated like the bull they kept out back.

EIGHTEEN

GUNS AT THE READY, ERIC and Ray traveled through the wooded area running parallel to the dirt road until the foliage grew too thick for passage. After checking both ways, they hesitantly stepped onto the open path like wading into frigid waters. It was foolish to be so exposed, but the one thing working in their favor was the road was winding and choked with vegetation. They'd hear an approaching vehicle from around the turn long before it would ever have a chance to spot them.

"C'mon." Ray said, taking the lead.

They moved in silence, partly from exhaustion over the recent events, but mostly to listen for trouble. About a half mile down, Eric broke that silence.

"Okay. I just gotta ask, 'cause I'm really confused about something."

Ray continued to scan the surrounding woods and the road ahead.

"What I don't get," Eric continued, "is why you don't want to go get this son-of-bitch. I might be able to understand it if you found

God and wanted to turn the other cheek, but—"

"Because I can't." The words came out barely above a whisper.

Eric moved closer. "What're you talking about? Of course you can."

Ray kept quiet and continued walking.

"Ray. C'mon, man. Talk to me."

Still no response. Eric quickened his pace and moved ahead of his brother to face him. Stare him in the eye. "Hey. Talk to me."

Ray slowed to a stop. He knew Eric wasn't going to let it go until he got some sort of answer. He opened his mouth to speak but the words didn't want to come. So he forced them out. "Up until last night, I thought I killed the man that murdered my wife. I did unspeakable things to him that did nothing but tear me right down to his level. A level that would've completely disgusted Rachel."

"I don't think so," Eric said. "I mean, given the circumstances I think she would've—"

Ray held up his hand. "Don't. Just … don't go there." He turned away and took a deep breath before continuing. "I thought killing him would make me feel better. Knowing I avenged her … made the wrong things right and all that bullshit. But it didn't. It just made me feel sicker." He paused again, carefully choosing his words. "Only recently have I been able to get Jacobs' screaming out of my head. Like fuckin' clockwork, it always comes late at night, in the dark, right before I'm about to fall asleep. Been haunting me for years. But for the past few months, it's finally gone quiet. So for me to go with you to get this guy, it isn't going to do anything but bring me right back to square one all over again. It's not gonna make me feel better. Not gonna bring me closure. And not gonna bring Rachel back."

"Well …" Eric said, "I just can't let it go like that. He has to be put down. 'Cause, like Rachel, I'm sure he's done this to plenty of other innocent people. And I'm not gonna allow that to happen anymore."

Ray met his brother's stare. After a long silence he sighed and looked away. He knew Eric was right.

"Look!" Eric said.

Ray turned back to him, thinking his brother was trying to further justify his point. Instead, he was pointing off into the woods.

"Over there. You see it?"

Ray's eyes narrowed. Then he nodded. "Yeah. Okay. Let's move."

Both men entered the wooded area. They crept ahead, weaving around trees before finally stopping at a line separating dense foliage from open pasture. Eric pulled out his mini-binoculars. Crouching for cover within the overgrowth, the men looked out into the large field.

Beyond the clearing sat a modest, single-story farmhouse, its wood paneling painted a cool, sky blue. It had a freshly trimmed lawn and beautiful bed of vibrant flowers lining its foundation. Bird houses and feeders hung from the trees in the front yard. A large, well-kempt garden sat in the lot beside it. Farther back was a standalone garage. A dirt driveway led around to the garage's entrance, which faced away from the house. Overall, it looked like the owners took great pride in their property.

"Garage. Over there," Eric said. "Whatcha think?" He handed his brother the binoculars.

Ray took them and sized up the building. Upon closer inspection, the old, gable-style garage wasn't in nearly as good shape as the house. In fact, it looked downright neglected, with its wood paneling weathered and rotten in parts. But the exterior wasn't their concern. What might be inside certainly was since it was large enough to house multiple vehicles. The side of the building facing them had two sets of large barn doors and a regular-sized door with a multipane window next to it. All access points were closed, sealed shut with large, shiny padlocks. Even the window was blacked out, probably painted over from the inside. "Considering all those padlocks, they got something valuable in there. Maybe there's another entrance around back that's not locked."

Both men scanned the area for any movement but found the place deserted and still.

"All right," Ray said. "Go for the garage. Move fast and stay sharp."

Stepping out into the open, the men were only a few yards into the field when a flash came from the wooded area at the end of the long driveway. More flashes, moving faster behind the foliage. Then they heard the engine of the approaching vehicle and quickly retreated for cover.

A shiny, red pickup emerged from the wall of trees and made its way up the winding dirt driveway. The truck looked new. Reliable. Fast.

"Well ain't our luck changing by the minute," Eric said.

They watched as the truck rolled to a stop beside the front of the house. The driver's door opened. Ray raised the binoculars for a closer look.

A young woman slid out from behind the wheel. A definite headturner, she wore tight jeans and an even tighter tank-top. Her dark ponytail danced across her tan shoulders as she made her way around the vehicle. Grabbing her purse and a bag of groceries off the passenger seat, she slammed the door shut with a bump of her hip, then headed for the front porch.

"Damn," Ray said.

"Let me see." Eric grabbed the binoculars. "Damn. Chick *is* hot."

"No. Look in her left hand."

Eric homed in on the truck keys dangling from her fingers. "Oh. Well, she's still hot." The woman dropped the keys into her purse and disappeared around the corner.

Ray groaned. "Things would've been so much easier if she just left them in the damn truck." He ran a hand through his hair and racked his brain for a plan. "Okay-okay-okay-okay-okay."

"It's not that hard," Eric said. "We knock on the door. When she answers, we calmly show her our guns and ask for the keys."

"And what if she refuses? What if she panics and does something stupid? Or what if someone else is in there with her? Like a kid?" Ray shook his head. "No. No guns."

"Look, we've already lost enough time. Which means we have to hightail it out of here. Now. So if you feel like going in there and giving her some song and dance that will make her magically give you the truck, have it. You've got five minutes. After that, I'm going in and taking the keys." Eric snapped open the wheel on his revolver and dumped the bullets in his palm. Giving them the once over to make sure there were no empties, he reloaded them back into the pistol. "I'm done. The gloves are off. This shit is about survival now. So no more bullshit."

"Fine." Ray stood and tucked his gun into his back waistband and covered it with his shirt tail. "You stay here. Watch for company. I'll handle it."

"I'm serious, Ray. Five minutes."

Ray ignored him and crossed over the natural barrier that separated shadowy treeline from brightly lit field.

NINETEEN

UPON ENTERING THE KITCHEN, THE woman was greeted by the ringing telephone mounted on the far wall. She tossed her purse on the table and the groceries on the counter. Moving to answer the call, she did a double take out the window above the sink. Her eyes narrowed.

In the distance, a man was crossing the meadow and making his way toward her house.

Surprised by the sight, she let out a subtle "Huh ..." and watched him move closer.

Over her shoulder, the phone continued ringing for her attention.

"All right. All right. Hold your horses." She turned and snatched the phone from its cradle.

Passing various windows, Ray snuck a peek inside for any sign of trouble but saw none. He ascended the porch steps and their wood planks creaked under his weight. Taking a deep breath, he rapped on the windowed door then padded back to edge of the porch to keep his distance and avoid coming off as threatening.

Light footsteps were heard on the other side of the door then the sheer curtain pulled back. Ray smiled and waved. The curtain dropped back into place and the door creaked open about a foot. Ray waved again at the woman peering out and immediately felt like a moron for doing so.

"Hi," she said.

"Ma'am."

Taking a step closer, Ray was caught off guard by the woman's natural beauty. Her big, brown eyes and warm smile reminded him so much of Rachel he suddenly got butterflies in his stomach.

God, I miss her.

"Can I help you?"

Lost in the blissful memory of his wife, Ray didn't answer. The woman waited and a hint of nervousness crept into her smile. Her eyes darted down to make sure his hands were visible. And empty. His lack of response caused the opening at the door to shrink. The jarring creak from its movement finally snapped Ray from his daze.

"Ah. Yeah. I'm sorry," he said. "Guess I'm just a little bit out of it. Um ... my car broke down on the road back there ..." Ray thumbed over his shoulder and hoped there actually was a road back there. "And I was wondering if maybe ... I could use your phone to call for a tow?"

It took every ounce of willpower for Ray not to glance over her shoulder and into the house to see if she was alone.

"Ya know," she said. "I don't get much visitors around here. Most people only stumble across me if they get lost. Heck, sometimes even my closest neighbors have a hard time finding my place."

He glanced out into the yard. "I bet. But it sure is beautiful. And I'm sure solitude is what makes it such a peaceful place to live." *C'mon, now. Don't lay it on too thick.*

The woman chuckled. "Thanks." She gave him the once over again then shook her head. "God, where're my manners?" Stepping back, she held the door open for him. "Now how can I turn away a person in need. C'mon in."

Ray stepped past her and into the entryway, facing the interior of the house. While she turned to close the door behind her, he did a quick survey of the place, something he'd mastered given his criminal past. To his left, a long hallway with three closed doors—two on the left and a third at the end. In front of him, the living room: two large windows on the far wall and a solid wooden door to the left—probably the backdoor. To the right of the living room was a connecting room ... the dining room, evidence of that being the fancy chair and polished edge of the table glimpsed in its open doorway.

The kitchen was to his right. Another open doorway at the far end of it must've led to the dining room to the left. Sink was straight ahead. And a kitchen table with four chairs to the right.

They seemed alone, unless someone was behind one of those closed doors down the hall.

Once the front door shut, the woman extended a hand to Ray. "I'm Jessie."

He shook it. "Nice to meet you, Jessie. I'm Ray."

She nodded likewise then pointed to the kitchen's open doorway. "Phone's that-a-way."

Ray entered the kitchen and saw incense burning on the counter. Vanilla. "Mmm. Smells good in here."

"Thanks."

He snuck a glance at her open purse on the table. It was nestled atop a pile of junk mail, newspapers, and magazines.

"There she is," Jessie said. She pointed at a phone mounted on the wall by the entry to the dining room ... miles away from the purse.

"Ah. Thank you."

He picked up the handset as she went to the counter to unpack the groceries. Punching nine numbers on the keypad, he paused on the tenth and glanced over his shoulder. She had her back to him.

He quickly pressed the receiver, voiding the call. After a click, the dial tone sounded and he pressed the phone to his ear to avoid tipping her off. His eyes shifted to the purse. His plan was simple, maybe too simple: snatch the keys without her noticing and say he better get back to his car to wait for the tow truck. Once outside, he'd wave Eric over, they'd hop in her truck, and take off before she even had a chance to process what was happening.

A sudden panic crawled up from the pit of his stomach.

What if she took the keys back out of her purse? Like to unlock the front door? If so, they could've been placed anywhere!

At his ear, the dial tone abruptly stopped. Next would be the automated voice telling him the phone was off the hook. Then the nails-on-a-chalkboard howler tone warning all within range the line was about to be temporarily disabled. If Jessie heard either coming from the earpiece, she'd know something was amiss.

Ray gently placed the phone back on its cradle. "Busy. I'll try back in a minute. I mean, if that's okay with you?"

"Sure. No problem."

He nodded to the kitchen table. "Mind if I sit for a second? Been on my feet all morning and sure could use the rest."

She motioned for him to take a seat. Ray went to the table and, again, peeked into the open purse as he passed. He sat in the far chair, placing his back against the wall but still remaining within reach of the handbag. His quick glimpse did little to calm the knot that slid tighter in his belly. There was just too much clutter inside to tell if the keys were even there. Remembering his brother's ultimatum, he checked his watch, unsure of when his five minutes had started. It was time to move quickly, before things went awry, especially if Eric knocked on the door with gun in hand.

Under the table, his nerves took over one leg, bouncing it like a jackhammer. He had to (somehow) get Jessie to step out of the kitchen for a minute or two, just long enough to search the purse.

"Want something to drink?"

Lost in thought, Ray jumped at the sound of her voice. Her back was still to him, luckily missing his nervous reaction. "Sure. Sure."

"I'm not a coffee drinker," she continued. "But I could make us some tea."

"Sounds good."

"Great. We can have a cup then you can try your call afterwards. Okay?"

"Okay."

Jessie stuck the teapot full of water on the stove and fired up a burner. "Here," she said, striding to the table. "Let me get that stuff out of your way." She scooped up her purse, along with the magazines, newspapers, and junk mail, and carried all to the far counter. Way out of reach.

Ray instantly deflated and swallowed back the loud sigh wanting to escape.

Jessie leaned against the counter, crossed her arms, and stared at Ray. With forearms pressed high on her naval, her breasts were pushed up even more, augmenting her already ample cleavage in the tight tank top. "So ...?"

Ray cleared his throat and fought to stay focused on her eyes. After all, he was still a man and she was a beautiful young lady. One that sure as shit knew how to use her sexuality to tongue-tie a man. Which, truth be told, made Ray a little suspicious. This wasn't a farmer's daughter scene from some porno. She was far too trusting to invite a complete stranger into her house. And that business about calling for a tow he pulled out of his ass? How would he even know of a local number to call? How come she didn't ask him that? Maybe she thought he meant something like AAA. But still, why didn't she—

Stop it! Stay focused. Ray smiled. "So ...? What?"

She went to the table and sat across from him. "So what brings you all the way out here? To my part of the country, so to speak? I mean, before you broke down and all."

Ray thought carefully before answering, then shook his head and faked a sigh of disbelief. "It's a long story, Jessie."

"The water's gotta boil. We got time."

"Let's just say I can be a little stubborn sometimes."

She giggled. "Oh, let me guess. Too stubborn to stop and ask for directions? Typical guy thing?"

"Yeah. Something like that."

"Well, I have to say, you must be pretty pig-headed to end up all the way out here." She rose to retrieve cups and saucers from the cabinet.

"Speaking of ..." Ray said. "How do I get to I-35 from here? How lost am I, exactly?"

"I-35?" She giggled again. "Wow. You are pretty damn stubborn." She set the tea cups on the counter. "Let's put it this way, with all these little farm roads out here, it'd probably be easier if I just draw you a map how to get back."

Ray sighed in relief. "That would be so awesome. Thank you."

"No problem." She looked around the countertop for a moment, searching for something to write with, then shook her head. "I got a pen and notepad in the guestroom. Be right back."

Holy shit! How the hell did that just happen? Ray tried to keep his cool and not show his extreme gratitude for the sudden change of luck.

Then, the moment Jessie left the kitchen, he bolted from his chair and went for her purse.

Eric sprung to his feet with pistol drawn. "Oh, shit." He raised the binoculars for another look.

In the distance, a beat-up and mud-caked, yellow Jeep Wrangler appeared, plowing its way up the long driveway, its fabric top and plastic windows rippling in the wind. It veered from the graveled path and made a wide arc around the house toward the backyard. In a matter of moments, he'd completely lose sight of the vehicle once it moved behind the home.

He needed to get in closer. Avoid detection. See if the driver was a threat. But in order to do so, he had to move now. Using the trees as cover, he bolted through the woods curving around the property that would lead him directly to the back of the house.

Ray dug through the purse. The keys had to be in there. His eyes darted back and forth between the handbag and the front entryway, watching for any sign of Jessie.

He clawed through its contents, past the old shopping lists, wrappers, cosmetics, and hair brush, praying the entire time to hear the jingle of keys.

His heart jack hammering in his chest, Eric raced through the woods, whipping around trees and over uneven terrain. The binoculars fell from his grasp, but he kept moving. No time to stop. Pushing on, he fought to control his labored breathing and heavy steps to keep his approach stealthy—or, in case either gave him away, to have enough wind left in him for a fight.

The purse dropped to the counter. There was plenty of crap inside but the keys didn't seem to be there. Ray scanned the room for some other place they could be. A peg on the wall. A glass bowl full of pocket change. A hook embedded under a cabinet to hang them on. Or maybe accidentally mixed in with the stack of junk mail from the table. He went to the pile and continued his search.

The Jeep slid into Eric's blind spot between the back porch and the old garage. He still needed to cover about a hundred yards of the curving, wooded perimeter before he'd catch sight of the driver. By then, it'd probably be too late. They'd already be inside the house.

Shifting gears, Eric took a more direct approach, charging out of the woods and into the open field, hoping the garage would obstruct his reckless advance.

With pencil and notepad in hand, Jessie entered the kitchen and stopped dead in her tracks.

Ray sat at the table. A thin sheen of sweat coated his face.

"You ... you okay?"

Trying to play it cool and failing miserably, Ray shrugged. "Yeah. Why?"

"'Cause, no offense, you're sweating like a pig." Jessie moved past him and placed the pencil and pad on the counter beside the knife block near the sink. "You want some water? Or maybe an aspirin or something?"

Ray stared at her in silence, ignoring the questions.

The charade was over. His brother was right. It was time to take the keys.

He rose from the table.

Nauseous and completely winded, Eric finally reached the garage and slammed against it. He winced at his clumsiness but focused on the immediate need to catch his breath and avoid throwing up. How in the hell was he so out of shape? Hunched over, hands on his knees, he sucked in air while his heart nearly erupted from his chest. After a few moments, he regained enough composure to stand upright.

A car door slammed opposite the garage.

Eric peeked around the corner and saw the parked Jeep aimed at the house. There was movement near the back porch but the vehicle obscured his view of it. The creaking of a knob was followed by the pop and twang of a screen door's rusty spring.

Eric almost rushed forward for a better look, using the Jeep as cover, then thought better of it. Its rear plastic windows were too opaque from all the mud to make out if someone else remained inside the vehicle.

The backdoor slammed shut with a loud crack.

Realizing it was too late, Eric slid back behind the corner of the garage to figure out his next move.

"Ray, what's the matter?" Jessie slowly pedaled back until pinned against the counter.

Ray inched toward her. "Look," he said, softly. Calmly. "I'm really sorry to have to do this, but I need to know where your—"

A door creaked open on the far side of the house then slammed shut. Ray spun toward the noise then looked at Jessie for an answer.

She shook her head and shrugged, looking genuinely concerned over the sound.

"My husband's out of town," she whispered.

Quickly realizing one of those backwood apes could have followed them to the house, Ray slid up beside Jessie to offer protection.

Eric figured storming the house was now too risky, especially without knowing who the driver of the Jeep was. It could be someone completely harmless. A kid brother. Hot roommate. An old grandma. Whoever. Let Ray continue his hustle inside and, if this new arrival wasn't someone so benign, Eric was still within earshot to help. Until then, he felt the need to do the obvious: check the garage. If it contained a vehicle with the keys in the ignition, he could put an end to all this other bullshit.

Of course, any plan of sneaking into the garage was foiled by the shiny padlocks clipped to each door. Still, Eric pulled the handles on both entrances, hoping the safety hasps would provide enough slack, especially at the bottom of either door, for him to slip through.

But the doors moved less than a half inch before snapping to a stop. Eric shoved them back and leaned against the wall nearest the blacked out window.

He checked his watch to see how much time had been wasted.

At the window just over his shoulder, where a portion of the black paint had been scratched away, a bloodshot eye continued watching his every move.

TWENTY

HEAVY FOOTSTEPS DREW CLOSER FROM the living room. Both Ray and Jessie stood frozen at the sink, waiting, their backs flush with the counter and eyes glued on the far entryway.

"You sure your husband's not home early?" Ray whispered.

"Dead sure. He just called me from Albuquerque right before you knocked on my door."

Ray slid a hand behind him and gripped the pistol. Jessie snatched a butcher knife from the wooden block and held it at the ready.

The tea kettle whistled, blowing steam from its spout and letting off a nerve-shattering shriek that grew louder, more insistent, with each passing second.

Ray grimaced and strained to hear the approaching steps over the pot's screeching.

After what felt like an eternity, the mystery guest finally revealed himself. A man with coke-bottle glasses, a crown of long greasy hair, and thick, bushy sideburns stepped out from around the corner.

Pork Chop.

Behind the thick specs, his watery eyes shifted between Ray and Jessie then to the squealing teapot at his side. He held up a finger for them to wait a sec then reached over and removed the kettle from the hot coil.

A welcome silence slowly fell over the room.

"Ahh, much better," Pork Chop said, almost to himself. Then to Ray and Jessie, "Well, howdy ya'll!"

Ray slid his finger into the revolver's trigger guard. He waited for Jessie's signal the man was a threat before revealing the gun.

"What are *you* doing here?" she asked the man and lowered the knife.

To Ray, her tone seemed more annoyed than scared. It still wasn't enough to determine if real trouble had entered the room.

Pork Chop threw back his head and chortled. "Well shit, baby girl! Why didn't ya tell me you already had him *in* the house?"

Ray did a double take at Jessie, trying to read her. Had he misunderstood the man's words?

Jessie flashed a smile. "'Cause I wasn't done playin' with the fucker yet." She turned and swung the knife at Ray. The blade sliced the air, missing his jugular by an inch.

Retreating into the corner, Ray whipped out his gun and aimed it at Jessie's face—her once beautiful features quickly morphed into something feral. Demonic.

She blocked the far exit of the kitchen leading to the dining room while Pork Chop barred the opposite one. Ray was trapped between the two.

A decorative rolling pin and large spice rack hung on the wall next to Pork Chop. Eying Ray and grinning, he slowly lifted the pin off its mount, sized it up, then gripped it like a club. "Yep. This is gonna do just fine."

Both took a step toward Ray, who swung his aim back and forth at them.

"Stop!" Ray commanded.

They only smiled and moved closer. Did these lunatics not see the loaded gun pointed at them?

They advanced another step.

"I said stop! What the fuck is wrong with you people!?"

Eric peeked at the house from around the garage. The backdoor was still closed with no movement at any of the windows. There was still zero signs of trouble, but things were taking way too long inside. And not knowing anything about the newcomer made him extremely uneasy. He ducked back against the garage's blacked-out window and checked his watch again. His index finger tapped the pistol's trigger guard.

Screw it. It was time to go in.

"Sorry, Ray. Something just don't feel right and I ain't about to—"

The window exploded around him. Razor shards of glass flew over his head and shoulders. A pair of massive arms sprung out of the opening and clamped under his armpits and around his chest, capturing him in a mighty bear hug. Rancid, hot breath snorted in his ear and blew over the back of his neck, raising goosebumps across his entire body.

Eric pinwheeled his own arms out and caught the window frame, barely stopping himself from being yanked back into the darkness. As his assailant's hold briefly loosened—readjusting for a better grip—Eric took advantage of the moment by squirming free and dropping straight down. The large hands swiped through the air to catch him but missed by mere inches.

Eric hit the ground and rolled out of his attacker's reach. It took a second to regain his bearings, but when he did he aimed and fired two shots into the darkness beyond the shattered window to prevent the beast inside from stepping out into the light.

Everyone in the kitchen turned to the gunshots outside.

Then Jessie spun to Pork Chop, her crazed look softening.

"What?" Pork Chop said. "I told ya there was two of 'em, girl! But, nooooo … you just wanted to fuck around with *this* one."

Panic washed across Jessie's face. "Oh, Precious!" She raised both hands to her cheeks and let off an ear-piercing scream like a woman completely devoured by madness.

Ray swung the gun at her and shifted away, carelessly stepping closer to Pork Chop. Jessie ducked around the corner, rushing to the other side of the house by way of the dining room.

Pork Chop took advantage of the distraction and lunged at Ray with the rolling pin. Ray whipped the gun at him, but Pork Chop was faster.

Swinging his makeshift bat, he struck the pistol full force as if bases were loaded. There was a loud clank of wood against metal as the gun flew out of Ray's hand and landed across the room on the linoleum floor.

Before Ray could defend himself, the rolling pin sliced the air on its backswing. It slammed against Ray's skull with a sickening crack and snapped his head to the side. The blow sent him stumbling. The room spun and clouds of ink swirled his vision. He bounced off the counter. Pork Chop caught him on the rebound by the shirt collar and heaved him across the kitchen.

Ray landed hard on the table. The impact surged through his bones and left him even more dazed. He lay there as vulnerable as a flipped turtle. Eyes fluttering, he slowly raised his head and caught a distorted vision of Pork Chop climbing onto the table with the rolling pin in hand, a maniacal grin stretching across the man's twisted face.

Eric wiped the stinging sweat from his eyes and scrambled to his feet. He kept the pistol trained on the garage's shattered window, waiting for his attacker to reveal himself.

Besides the dust kicked up by the commotion swirling within the sunlight, there was no other movement at the window. Just a wall of darkness where all light eerily failed to penetrate.

Realizing his gunshots had boldly announced his presence, Eric knew it was time to go and get his brother.

Straddling his dazed victim, Pork Chop placed the rolling pin over Ray's throat and slowly pressed down.

Ray felt his windpipe begin to cave and panicked, instinctively tucking his chin and drawing up his shoulders in an attempt to re-distribute the blunt force across his collarbone or upper chest. His face grew flushed and he gasped for air. His legs kicked wildly, try-ing to buck his attacker off. Seizing Pork Chop's wrists, he yanked down, hoping the motion would snap the man's grip from either side of the pin and throw him off balance. When all else failed, he tried to push up on the rolling pin and suck in a deep breath.

But nothing worked. His final act was primal—clawing for his attacker's eyes.

Pork Chop simply leaned back, out of range from the gnarled fingers swiping for his face.

Ray opened his mouth to scream but nothing sounded.

Pork Chop shushed him, pressed down harder, and emphasized the words, "Just. Go. To. Sleep."

Ray's struggle, frantic at first, now grew feeble. His arms dropped to his side. Blood seeped from the knot at his temple caused by the rolling pin strike. The crimson drops dotted the kitch-en table's polished surface.

Pork Chop saw the blood and licked his lips. "Oahhhh ... now, don't you move." He leaned in, crushing Ray with his full body weight. Then his tongue slid out and flickered serpent-like while lapping the blood at Ray's wound.

With his head pinned to the side, Ray was oblivious to the repul-sive act, even with Pork Chop whispering, "You taste sooo good," in his ear. He was far too busy fighting for the single breath needed to remain conscious until help arrived. That is, if Eric had even spotted the man's arrival from across the field.

Ray was on the verge of surrender ... which meant certain death. His eyes rolled up in their sockets. With back arching in a final attempt to shove his attacker off, the necklace he so cherished slid out from beneath his shirt collar.

Pork Chop did a double take at the piece of jewelry attached to it. He dropped a forearm across the rolling pin to keep the pressure steady and free up a hand. The move slightly redistributed the weight to Ray's advantage, allowing him to sneak a gulp of air.

Pork Chop lifted the necklace and leaned in closer. Inches from Ray's face, he stared at Rachel's wedding band on the end of the silver chain. Squinting behind his thick glasses, Pork Chop struggled to read the inscription engraved on the ring's underside. "My life ... my love ..."

Hearing those words, Ray's eyes slid down and locked on Pork Chop.

"... now and forever," Pork Chop continued, smiling. "Well, ain't that sweet. Now gimme!" He pulled at the necklace to take the ring.

A rage shot through Ray, igniting every muscle in his body needed to explode into action. He lurched up and headbutted Pork Chop's nose.

A sickening crack of broken cartilage sounded. Dropping the rolling pin, the man screamed and scooted off Ray. His hands cupped his shattered nose as blood dripped between his trembling fingers. With glasses askew, Pork Chop teetered on the table's edge.

Now it was Ray's turn to attack. He kicked with all his might and landed a solid blow to the chest.

Pork Chop rocketed back and slammed against the wall-mounted spice rack. Its bottled contents shattered upon impact and not only sent a choking cloud into the air but glass shards into his back. What didn't puncture flesh dropped to the floor at his feet and mixed with the various spices dusting the ground. Clawing at the agonizing pain in his lats and shoulders, Pork Chop stumbled forward on rubbery legs until they unhinged.

He folded and dropped to his knees, landing with a sickening crunch atop the broken glass. The man shrieked as the razor-like shards pierced the thin layer of nerves and grinded into his bony kneecaps. Then an array of spices—from sea salt and cumin to black pepper and cayenne—entered his wounds. Once that crescendo of pain reached full effect, Pork Chop squealed and bounced across the floor like it was mined with hot coils.

Ray slid off the table and landed on the ground with a heavy thud. Rolling onto his side and clutching his throat, he continued gasping for air. With each gulp that filled his lungs, the darkness around him retreated and, more importantly, his pistol lying on the floor by the sink came sharply into focus. He flipped onto his belly and glanced over at Pork Chop.

Frantically brushing his kneecaps like they were on fire, the man had long ribbons of bloody snot stretching from his nose and chin that swayed back and forth with his jerky movements. Pork Chop locked eyes with Ray, who immediately looked over at the gun … and inadvertently gave his intentions away.

Knowing he was closer to the revolver, Pork Chop flashed a bloody smile.

Ray rose to all fours and lunged forward but Pork Chop already had the lead, reaching the revolver first and snatching it off the ground. He swung and took aim. Ray shoved the pistol up and away as the round meant for his face blew a hole in the ceiling. Sheetrock dust rained upon them. Each man fought for control of the weapon but Ray was the weaker of the two, still gasping for breath. Pork Chop threw an elbow into his opponent's face and knocked him away.

Howling in victory, he rose to his bloody knees and drew a bead on Ray's bowed head. "Sayonara, fuck face!"

Two shots exploded in the kitchen.

The first blew out the elbow on Pork Chop's raised gun arm. The weight of the revolver in his hand made his arm fold in the opposite direction. Held together only by thin pieces of sinew and stretched flesh, the limb swung to the floor like a pendulum, splattering blood across his feet and pants leg.

The second shot punched a hole in his throat, blowing apart his all-too prominent Adam's apple. Escaping air hissed from the entry wound then blood bubbled out. Pork Chop clutched his neck with his good hand and frantically swallowed in a futile attempt to stop the wave of blood filling his windpipe.

Standing in the far entryway, Eric lowered his smoking gun and ran into the kitchen.

While drowning in his own blood, Pork Chop thrashed against the lower cabinets. Eric rushed him and stomped his gun hand. He pinned it to the floor and shattered the bones to prevent the trigger finger from getting off a wild round then shoved the muzzle of his .357 into Pork Chop's head, looked away with a grimace, and pulled the trigger. The snap of the hammer caused a muffled gelatinous pop, then Pork Chop fell over dead, his singed hair smoking from the muzzle flash.

Finally out of immediate danger, Ray collapsed on his back, his chest hitching, sucking in precious air.

Eric pried the gun from Pork Chop's rubbery grasp and asked Ray, "You okay?" Considering the man's bloody and beaten state, it was a dumb question but still a natural one to ask. "Can you stand?"

Ray nodded. Eric helped him to his feet and propped him against the counter.

"Jesus, Ray. What the fuck happened here? Where's the girl?" He pointed at Pork Chop. "What did he do to her?"

Ray shook his head and croaked out, "She's one of 'em." He grabbed his gun, reclaiming it from Eric, and fumbled for the bul-

MATT KURTZ

lets in his pocket to reload. "We're in their goddamn house."

TWENTY-ONE

SHE JUMPED AT THE GUNSHOTS from inside the house while fighting back the scream that wanted to erupt. Still, Jessie pushed ahead in a mad dash across the yard toward the old garage to check on her Precious. It wasn't her intention to abandon Cousin Francis with Ray back in the kitchen, but she panicked hearing the original two shots coming from the direction of the garage.

Precious might have been in danger.

Seconds earlier, she'd made her way out of the house and almost crossed paths with the other man, his gun drawn, rushing to enter the back door. He must have been Ray's brother, the one she was warned about. She hid behind the woodpile until he passed, then continued on.

Outnumbered, Francis was probably dead because of her somewhat selfish reaction. After all, a rolling pin was no match against a gun.

Rounding the corner of the garage, she fumbled with a set of keys then singled one out and inserted it into the padlock attached to the door next to the shattered window. Before she could pop the lock, a hand clasped over hers. She gasped and spun around.

It was Lew, with Red and Skeeter over his shoulder. All three were armed—Lew and Red with their shotguns; Skeeter with his straight razor.

The old man let go of her hand, pointed his chin at the garage door, and shook his head. "Not yet."

"I have to see if he's okay," she said. "Have to—"

"We already checked him. He's fine. So just leave him be until we really need that bull in the china shop."

Jessie thought it over for a moment before nodding.

Lew took the key ring from her and stepped away to sneak a peek at the house.

Jessie shivered from the massive adrenaline spike, goosebumps sprouting along her arms and shoulders. When her nipples poked through the tight tank top, Red huffed and threw his hands up in the air.

"Jesus, girl," he said, unbuttoning his shirt. "What'd we tell ya 'bout dressing like that with your titty meat all hangin' out?" He shrugged off his shirt, revealing his mangled flesh underneath.

His back and shoulders were covered in crisscrossing scar tissue and raised dots resembling cigarette burns. Some appeared recent, freshly scabbed. Whiteheads dotted the few patches of skin porous enough to cultivate acne. Although his arms were thick and muscular, his torso was flabby and sagging like he'd recently shed a ton of weight. His pale, freckled chest and downturned nipples looked more fitting for an old hound after suckling one too many litters. He offered his shirt to Jessie. "Put it on before a tit pops out. We got work to do now."

She took the top and slipped it on.

Lew returned to the group, his focus on Jessie. "So they in there?"

"Yeah," she said. "Francis, too."

"We heard some shots," Red said.

Skeeter nodded. "Yeah, ya think he got 'em?"

"When Francis came in, I don't think he had his guns."

The old man sighed and shook his head. "Why did the dumbass show up unarmed? We warned him about these two! What the fuck is wrong with this family?" He did a quick double take at Red, just now noticing the man was shirtless.

Lew eyed the pasty, zit-splotched skin and flabby man-boobs tipped with puffy, pepperoni nipples, all blown out in the bright sunlight. "Christ Almighty! Don't you have another shirt in your truck? Spare me the sight of your bitch-tits before I fuckin' puke! We're about to go to war and you wanna prance around half nekkid like some fairy? Go get something to cover yourself with!"

Red stood planted, glaring at the old man in defiance. After a long, awkward moment, he said, "Aight then," and spit a wad of chew … which landed directly on Skeeter's pants leg.

"Awe, c'mon now!" Skeeter yelled, and wiped at the glistening, brown stain. Before he could voice his objection any further, Lew clamped a hand over the young man's mouth.

"Shut that hole, boy," he told Skeeter. "And let's get ready to flush 'em out!"

The living room curtains snapped closed one after the other.

"They're definitely out there," Eric yelled to Ray over his shoulder. "Just saw someone crouching behind the Jeep. Think it's that orangutan that was driving the black pickup." Eric moved to the backdoor to check its deadbolt.

In the kitchen, Ray held a wet washcloth to the knot on his head and sighed. "Just make sure we're on lockdown 'til we figure something out." He turned back to the counter and dumped Jessie's purse onto it. Now able to do a more thorough search, he rummaged through the items. Inhaling sharply, he found the key ring and snatched it up. The ring only contained a few house keys and one that looked like it went to a pair of handcuffs.

The truck key was missing. Thinking it might've somehow fallen off the ring, he did another search of the contents but still found nothing.

Jessie must have removed it as a precaution. Insurance so they wouldn't be able to take her truck. He looked around the kitchen, knowing the single key could be anywhere in the house. He threw the purse across the room and exhaled.

Quickly sidestepping the window above the sink, he moved to the modest display of liquor bottles at the far end of the counter and poured himself a shot of whiskey. He glanced over his shoulder to check if he was alone, then slammed it. The liquid burned going down, its heat jump starting his brain which demanded more. So he poured himself another.

"You find the keys?" Eric said behind him.

Ray jumped and almost dropped the shot glass. He kept his back to his brother.

Eric craned his neck to see what Ray was hiding. "Oh, for shit's sake! Really? Now!?"

"Leave me alone." The words came out more like a growl. "Because of you, I hit a dirt wall going fifty miles-an-hour, been shot at more times today than I have in my entire life, and nearly strangled to death ... *twice*. Today *ain't* been too great. I deserve this. Just need a little something to take the edge off. So shut the hell up." Ray slammed the shot, capped the bottle, and turned over the glass, leaving it on the counter.

Eric watched him. Waited. "Are you really cool, man? 'Cause I need to know I can trust you. That you're not gonna be dealing with all this by getting shitfaced and—"

Ray held up his hand, silencing him. "I told you ... I'm fine. Finish your sweep of the house. Make sure it's locked down tight. I'll check him," he nodded at Pork Chop's corpse. "See if he has the keys to the Jeep on him."

It took a moment for Eric to respond. He was still studying Ray to see if his head was really in the game or if he was just trying to get some alone time with the bottle. "Okay. Holler if you see anything." He left the kitchen.

Ray stepped around the crimson puddle seeping out of Pork Chop and knelt beside the corpse. When he turned the body over to check his back pockets, he heard a wet bubbling noise. Ray grimaced then held his breath and sped up his search for the keys as the man's bowels continued to release like slow flowing lava.

In the narrow hallway, Eric inched forward, the floorboards creaking underfoot. The two doors on his left were closed, as well as the one at the end.

With revolver raised, Eric paused by the first door and strained to hear any signs of danger coming from the other side.

Repositioning his stance, he gave the knob a quick turn and kicked the door open, letting it swing back and slam against the wall in case someone was hiding behind it.

His eyes immediately clicked to the window across the small room. It was closed and he'd check the lock on it momentarily, but first needed to give the room the once over.

There was an open, shallow closet, one without a door and mostly barren. A bookcase of various knick-knacks, CDs, and dog-eared paperbacks. Corner desk. Small dresser. A neatly made twin bed.

Eric peered under it to make sure someone wasn't hiding there and only spotted a ratty pair of slippers and a few dust bunnies.

Okay. This room could be checked off the list. But first …

He strode to the window to check its latch. Even with the sheer curtains drawn, he made sure to stay out of sight, standing flush with the wall.

The window was locked.

The next door led to the master bedroom. Queen-size bed with an oak headboard and footboard. Two nightstands. Triple dresser with mirror. A vanity. Over-stuffed chair in the corner. The closet had dual sliding doors. Inside was a mix of men and women's clothing, neatly divided and well organized.

Eric checked behind the clothes then under the bed and thankfully didn't find some bloodthirsty, bucktoothed Bubba staring back at him.

Overall, the room was neat. Well-kempt. Locked window. Drawn curtains. Check.

As he approached the last door at the end of hall, a chill slithered up his spine. Something felt off. His hand hovered over the brass knob, then pulled away. He leaned in and listened.

Faint music came from the other side. It sounded compressed. Tinny. Distorted. Like coming out of headphone speakers or a small transistor radio. Eric stepped back and aimed his gun at the door.

There were two possibilities. Either Jessie heard Ray's knock at the front door and set the headphones down with music still playing … or there was someone on the other side of the door right now, jamming out. If the music was cranked up loud enough on the headphones, the listener would be oblivious to the assault and gunfire that took place earlier.

Hoping for the former, he twisted the knob, kicked the door inward, and dropped to a shooting stance.

Eric drew a bead on the seated figure opposite him. Then his eyes tore away from the person and danced wildly in their sockets over the surrounding horrors within the room.

TWENTY-TWO

"R-R-RAY! GET OVER HERE! NOW!"

Wiping the blood from his hands, Ray threw the dish towel aside and ran down the hall toward his brother's voice.

"What? What is it?" he said, coming up behind Eric.

Eric kept his pistol trained on the seated figure as Ray stepped up beside him. It was only then Ray got a complete view of the room.

Unlike the rest of the house, this room showed the true face of the people they were dealing with.

It was a den of depravity. A slaughterhouse. The walls appeared to be finger painted with blood. Huge smiley faces, gibberish words, and weird symbols were written in the dried, rusted hue, making it look like some kindergartener's artwork from hell. Flies swarmed the air. The putrid smell of spoiled meat and shit assaulted their senses. A bed shoved against the wall had its rumpled sheets hardened with dried blood and smeared feces. The surrounding floorboards were black and warped from absorbing bodily fluids dripped from the gore-soaked bedding. A low hanging dome light stretched down from the ceiling and hung over the bed. Atop the wooden dresser sat a large mallet and a wide array of knives, screwdrivers, pliers, saws, and flaying tools. Dual doors to a sliding closet lined one side of the room while the adjacent wall had a window covered with a white sheet, its fabric allowing light in while still providing privacy for the horrors taking place within.

His mouth agape, Ray retreated a few steps and bumped into Eric then whipped his gun at the person seated in the rocking chair. Whomever it was, they were draped from head to toe in a bed sheet like some homemade Halloween ghost costume minus the eyeholes. Once white, the sheet was now stained with large patches of rusty brown. Dried blood. The Ghostman wore headphones over the sheet and the music was cranked up so loud that Beethoven's 9th Symphony could be heard blaring out of its tiny speakers.

"Raise your hands," Eric commanded. "And get up slowly!"

Both men waited. The cloaked figure sat frozen. Even the rocking chair failed to sway.

Ray visually followed the headphone cord and saw it plugged into a vintage record player sitting a few feet away. Keeping his pistol aimed at the Ghostman, he shuffled over and flipped off the turntable. The light illuminating the electronic display went dark and the phonograph slowed to a stop, its symphony frozen in time.

Silence filled the room.

"Hey, asshole," Eric said. "I know you can hear me now. So get up. Slowly."

Still nothing.

"It's gotta be a dummy or something," Ray whispered.

Eric fired a shot into the figure's upper leg.

The bullet tore into the fabric, exited the thigh, and punched a dot into the plaster wall at the baseboard. The chair rocked slightly then creaked to a stop. There was no scream. No flinch of pain. And no fresh blood spreading beneath the sheet.

Eric lowered his gun. "Guess so." He strode across the room to unveil the figure. Was it some department store manikin? A wax figure? Maybe a scarecrow prop left over from Halloween? He grabbed the sheet and ripped it off. The action threw aside the headphones and stirred the dust in the room.

What lay underneath made Eric jump back and bury the lower half of his face in the crook of his elbow to avoid the stench.

Both men, the breath frozen in their lungs, turned away from the horrifying sight as a fresh wave of rot rode the room. They glanced at each other in disbelief then forced themselves to look back at the ghastly corpse.

The rotting man sat in the rocking chair. The top of his head had been sawed off, just above the brow. His skull, scalped and scraped clean, sat in its rightful place, only it was crooked and hanging over the edge of his forehead at a forty-five-degree angle. Large chunks had been torn from his neck and shoulders, teeth marks plainly visible around the trauma. His eyeballs were missing, replaced by dark, hollow sockets writhing with maggots. The jaw was slack, his mouth stretched wide in a silent scream. Both stomach and chest were open cavities, bite marks circling the rotten chasms. His sex appeared chewed off and most of the meaty parts of his legs and arms flayed to the bone. His entire body had been carved away like the carcass of a Thanksgiving turkey. Faded writing—a series of numbers and letters, either tattooed or drawn on with permanent marker—decorated the patch of gray, marbled flesh remaining on one of the forearms.

Ray stepped closer and studied the set of digits. Some sort of code? Passwords? Or maybe license plates.

Eric threw the sheet back over the corpse, partially out of respect, but mostly to conceal the god-awful stench. After checking the window lock—his original intention for entering the room—he wiped his hand on his pants leg and quickly returned to his brother's side.

"Ya know," Ray said, unable to look away from the cloaked

corpse. "This is *their* house. And a locked door or window don't mean shit when they have the keys to everything."

"Then we make a run for it." Eric glanced at the knot now scabbing on Ray's head. "You feelin' up to it?"

Ray nodded and the brothers moved down the hall for the living room. "The guy in the kitchen didn't have any keys so they might still be in his Jeep. Think we should try that first before checking out the garage."

"Well, let me just remind ya there's something big and pissed off in there. And it might take both of us to put it down. Along with most of our bullets. Just hope there ain't any more fuckers with it or we're really gonna be screwed."

Ray pulled back the curtain on the far living room window for a peek. The Jeep was parked about fifteen yards away. "Looks clear." He joined Eric at the windowless backdoor. "You reloaded?"

Eric held up his gun and nodded.

"Okay," Ray continued. "I move first. You cover me. And I'll check the Jeep."

"Sounds like a plan. But once we're both outside, we need to make sure we—"

The deadbolt in front of them flipped over.

Ray and Eric froze, both temporarily confused as to how it just unlocked itself. Then it quickly became quite obvious …

Someone was on the other side of the door.

The doorknob slowly turned, letting off a grating metallic squeak.

Ray padded back. Eric followed. Both trained their guns on the door as it creaked open a half inch or so, then paused. A shadow fell under its jam.

Eric fired first, dead center of the door, putting three slugs through it. Ray punctuated it with two rounds of his own. The bullets punched through the wood, splintering it.

Ray rushed forward and kicked the door shut, then flipped the deadbolt back and sought cover against the nearest wall. He grabbed a wooden chair sitting beside him, swung it around, and wedged its back under the door handle. The chair wasn't sturdy enough to stop someone from entering but at least it would offer some resistance, enough to sound a warning of any possible forced entry. Further barricading it would be foolish since the back door still had to remain an exit option, especially if the house got stormed from the other side.

Movement to the right caught Eric's attention. A shadow ran past both windows, continuing on toward the dining room and kitchen.

"Cover that door!" Eric told Ray then gave chase.

"Wait! Don't split up!"

Just as Ray finished his warning, one of the living room windows exploded inward.

TWENTY-THREE

BUCKSHOT SHREDDED THE CURTAINS AND spit glass into the room. A chunk of the wall next to Ray blew apart. He dropped to the floor and aimed his gun at the window as a cloud of sheetrock and splinters descended upon him.

Eric peeked in from the dining room and saw Ray on the ground dusting his hair, his head and shoulders powdered white. "Shit! You okay?"

"Oh, yeah. Couldn't be better!"

Eric glanced back into the kitchen and saw a shadow zip past the window above the sink. "Good. Then let's nail these fuckers!"

Rushing into the kitchen, Eric sidestepped the bloody corpse on the floor and peeked out the window.

No one was there.

The shadow spotted earlier had been heading toward the front of the house so he scrambled to meet them at the porch.

Pulling back the curtain on the front door, he caught a glimpse of a foot just as it disappeared around the far corner of the house. Again, too late.

"Dammit!"

Eric barreled down the hallway, hoping to stop them at a bedroom window. He entered the first room, checked outside, and saw no one.

Impatient, he ducked out and swung into the master bedroom. His eyes suddenly widened and he slid to a stop.

The window was open. The sheer curtains stirred gently in the breeze.

No. He checked the damn thing earlier and it was locked.

So, how could it be open now?

In the living room, Ray had his own breach to deal with. The shotgun blast had decimated most of the window, leaving only splintered sash bars and shards of glass embedded in the frame like a transparent row of shark's teeth.

Even with the glass missing, the window was far from an easy access. Because of the sloping landscape outside, the opening was about five feet off the ground, making it impossible for someone to just leap in. And if they tried to crawl through, they'd be slashed to ribbons or forced to break the remaining glass. Either case would provide ample warning of an attack.

Nevertheless, it still left it an extremely vulnerable point of entry, one that just needed a simple step stool and a gunstock to clear the jagged frame for safe passage.

The window needed to be guarded. It would be too tempting for one of those inbreds *not* to enter.

Ray quickly replaced his two spent bullets. Then, with gun pointed at the blowing curtains, he slowly rose and waited for someone stupid enough to poke their head inside for a look-see.

Remaining out of sight, Eric slammed the window in the master bedroom shut and flipped its lock. After a quick check under the bed, he turned to the closet and noticed one of the sliding doors was slightly open. It was only cracked an inch or so, which was more than enough for someone inside to be watching his every move.

Without warning, Eric raised his gun and fired three shots across the sliding doors before his cylinder clicked empty. He stared at the gun incredulously, realizing he'd forgotten to reload after shooting at the backdoor. "Shit!"

"Eric!" Ray called from the other room in a panic. "What's happening?!"

"It's all good! Just gimme a second, hon!"

His gun empty, Eric might as well have been standing there with his dick in his hand. Before he could be attacked, Eric charged forward and bum rushed the sliding doors.

Both panels flew inward—off their track—and slammed against the back of the closet, knocking clothes off their hangers and taking out the upper shelf.

With his pistol raised like a club, he peeled back both doors, ready to strike anyone underneath.

Only the closet was empty.

Out of breath, he stumbled back and began reloading his gun with the last of his bullets, steadying himself to move on to the next room.

The slaughter room.

Ray heard the three shots and dropped for cover. Once able to determine they hadn't been directed at him, he called out to check on his brother.

Eric calmly told him to hold on. Then, before Ray could press further about the gunfire, there was a loud crash as Eric plowed into the master bedroom closet.

Enough was enough.

Ray leaped to his feet and rushed to the entryway. He straddled both the living room and hallway, his attention constantly shifting between the shotgun-blasted living room window, the stretch of corridor ahead, and all the other surrounding windows that might make him an easy target.

"Eric!" he yelled down the hall, pistol at the ready, eyes scanning. "What was that? You okay or not!?"

Eric poked his head out of the room while reloading his gun. "Just peachy."

"Then quit fuckin' around and let's figure a way outta here."

"Fuckin' around? Oh, suuuuuure," Eric said, his head wildly bobbing. "I'm just having sooooo much fun here playing, ya know!"

The crunch of broken glass stole Ray's attention back to the living room. It came from just outside the shattered window.

Then a shadow stretched across its curtain.

Ray glided back into the room and raised his pistol.

Take cover, his mind screamed at him. *They're coming.*

He quickly slid behind the nearby recliner and, with gun raised, waited for a clean shot.

Eric didn't bother waiting for Ray. He shoved open the door to the slaughter room and entered, quickly passing the cloaked corpse seated in the chair. He made his way to the window and found it still locked.

And just like in the previous room, the sliding door to the closet was cracked open on one side, allowing a sliver of darkness to stare back at him. Had it always been like that? He kicked himself for not checking inside it earlier. Didn't matter now because this game of hide and seek was over.

Knowing the last of his bullets were loaded in his gun, he couldn't fire indiscriminately. Every shot had to count. Eric slowly advanced toward the closet to see who and what was inside.

"Help. Me."

The child's voice yanked Eric back and he stood frozen, his gun aimed at the closet where the soft words had escaped the dark opening.

"Please ..." it said.

His finger lifted off the trigger, but remained within its guard. Even if it was a child, it could still be one of *their* kids. And as fucked up as this clan was, their children were probably far from benign. If one were to spring out and attack, he wouldn't shoot it, but he'd sure as shit pistol whip it into submission. Catching one of them would be a great bargaining tool for safe passage.

Eric gazed into the strip of darkness and tried to make out anything within its void. Then with the gentlest tone he could muster, he said, "Okay. Why don't you come out here? I wanna see you."

"Can't. I'm tied up. Please. *Please*, Mister. Help me before they come back."

Eric sighed and tightened his grip on the pistol. It had to be a trap. Or else why would this kid only now be calling for help instead of doing it earlier when both he and Ray had been in the room?

Maybe the kid was drugged and just came to? So maybe it wasn't a trap? Maybe it was someone they kidnapped and had tied up in there. Like the son or daughter of the poor son-of-a-bitch carved up in the rocking chair just over his shoulder? What if they were about to do God knows what to this poor kid when Ray and Eric stumbled across their tranquil little abode?

"I want my mommy. Please."

Sucking in a deep breath, Eric knew what needed to be done. Time wasn't a luxury to be wasted anymore. He stepped forward, the floorboards creaking under his weight.

And he inched closer to the closet door. The cloaked corpse over his shoulder raised its stooped head and turned in his direction.

TWENTY-FOUR

HIS HEART NOW DRUMMING A triple beat, Ray kept cover behind the recliner and heard the crunch of broken glass outside again. He snuck a glimpse at the backdoor to make sure the wood chair was still firmly wedged under its handle then looked back to the window. A bead of sweat rolled from his hairline and down his brow, causing his eye to twitch. He ignored it and remained focused on the curtains blowing in the breeze. Someone was out there. About to reveal themselves.

An eerie silence fell across the room.

His scalp prickled. Definitely the calm before the storm.

He thumbed back the revolver's hammer and the cylinder rotated. The click it made was amplified a hundredfold by the deafening silence. Ray slowly exhaled and waited for the person outside to finally show their face.

Approaching with the revolver, Eric aimed at the closet and reached out with his other hand to slide open the door.

"Please, Mister. *Hurry.*"

Eric paused. No. The squirming in his gut told him none of this was right. He retreated a few steps and eyed the closet.

Follow that instinct.

"Hey, Ray!" he said, his eyes glued ahead. "I could use your help in here!"

Turning away from the window, Ray debated whether to answer or quietly get up and find his brother.

A response now would warn whoever it was outside of his presence, losing him the element of surprise and the opportunity to eliminate another threat.

"Ray!"

He waited. Then shook his head. "What's the problem?!"

Again, the crunch of broken glass outside. Ray swung back to the window.

"Don't know if there is one," Eric answered. "Not yet!"

"Well, I've got my own shit to deal with in here!"

No response.

"Eric?"

"Yeah?"

"Can you handle it yourself or not?"

Silence.

Ray's gut twisted. He and Eric should not be separated like this. If Lew and his messed up brood had intended to rid the brothers of their strength in numbers, they'd succeeded. He desperately needed to get Eric and figure out a new strategy since barricading themselves inside the house was never supposed to be a permanent plan. They needed to move. Be proactive. Fluid. Not trapped. Cornered like animals.

Ray rose from behind the recliner to go find his brother. He backed up slowly toward the hallway, his eyes ticking back and forth between the bullet-riddled door and shattered window. "Hey, Eric? I'm coming. So don't shoot my ass, okay?"

Before he could take another step, the second living room window exploded inward. Ray reeled back and swung his gun at the uproar.

Something large flew through the window in a shower of glass, snagging the curtains and ripping them off the rod. The object landed with a heavy thud that pounded the wooden floorboards beneath Ray's feet, buckling his knees.

His initial fear was someone had leaped through the window. But he'd caught sight of the object in mid-air—something large and square.

Pistol now aimed at the second broken window, he craned his neck and spotted the large cinderblock on the floor, a mosaic of shattered glass surrounding it. The chunk of cement lay behind the couch, part of a three-piece furniture set positioned near the middle of the room.

A voice floated in through the second window, taunting Ray. "Gonna get you, boy …"

A surge of adrenaline—brought on by anger, not fear—ignited within Ray. He strode over to the windows, gun whipping back and forth between the two, searching for whoever the voice belonged to so he could shut them up. Permanently.

Eric heard the commotion in the other room but kept his gun locked on the closet.

"Ray?!" he screamed without turning. "What the hell is—"

"Oh, God, Mister!" the child said. "That's them! They're coming! Please hurry!"

"Ah, fuck this!" Eric lunged forward, slid the door open, and swiped aside the clothes hanging inside the shallow closet. Seated against the opposite wall was a small figure cloaked in a blanket.

Eric ripped off the cover and stepped back.

It was no child seated on the closet's dingy floor.

The ventriloquist's dummy, monocled and dressed to the nines in a tuxedo, stared up at Eric with its mouth hanging slack, showing off its painted teeth. Eric kicked it aside to find the speaker that had to be projecting the voice. He saw nothing until glancing up.

It was then that his eyes nearly exploded from their sockets.

TWENTY-FIVE

LETTING HIS ANGER GET THE best of him, Ray foolishly stuck his head out the window for a quick peek but found no one around the glass-strewn perimeter. He realized his carelessness and ducked back inside to avoid making himself an easy target. With the wall pressed against his back, he tried to figure out his next move.

Then the light at the backdoor flickered. Someone had passed by, temporarily blocking the small beams of sunlight streaming in through the bullet holes. Ray threw his aim at the door, his eyes darting between the deadbolt and its handle, waiting to catch the slightest movement from either before opening fire.

In the closet, Jessie hung out of the small attic hatch above Eric's head. She held a butcher knife. "Hey there, sexy!" she said, childlike.

Stabbing down, she tried to ram the knife into the top of his skull.

Eric ducked.

The blade sliced the air and narrowly missed hacking off his ear.

Scrambling back, Eric tripped over his own feet and fell out of the closet. He threw out both hands to break his fall and his trigger finger extended out of the pistol's guard. As he hit the ground, the finger snapped.

The crack of bone was followed by a lightning bolt of pain shooting up his arm and exploding in his brain. Instinctively, he dropped the gun and buried his wounded hand into his chest.

Like a newborn crawling out of the womb, Jessie started her descent. With her upper body hanging out of the hatch, she braced her arms against the upper shelf and the wall above the door to support her weight.

Before even bothering to locate the gun at his side, Eric kicked the sliding doors with all his might. Both panels shot off the track and flew inward, clipping Jessie's head and arms hard enough to cause the doors to bounce back. Eric kicked them again on the rebound, hoping to stop her descent and pin her against the far wall, but she managed to pull herself to safety, back up into the opening.

He continued striking the panels until they became wedged inside the closet and their tops bisected the attic opening, barring any entrance from above. At least temporarily.

Eric grabbed for his gun and winced in pain after instinctively trying to curl his finger into the trigger guard. He quickly switched the revolver to his left hand where it felt awkward and clumsy, like trying to brake smoothly in a car using the opposite leg.

Scrambling to his feet, his heart pounding at jackhammer speed, he aimed the gun at the ceiling and tried to estimate Jessie's whereabouts.

Over his shoulder, the ghostly figure in the stained sheet silently rose from the rocking chair.

"C'mon, ya crazy bitch," Eric yelled above. "How 'bout you come down here and I'll show ya sexy?" His gun aimed high, he waited for a creak to give away her location and avoid wasting precious ammo.

Behind him, Skeeter ripped off the stained sheet and raised his straight razor.

Like it was happening in slow motion, Eric heard the sheet drop to the floor and felt its breeze blow over him. Before he could turn, Skeeter swung down, hacking into Eric's left shoulder. He pressed on the razor and slid the blade down across Eric's back, slicing through fabric and flesh.

Flailing wildly, Eric screamed and rocketed forward to escape the pain but had no place to go. He violently slammed into the wall and bounced back directly into the arms of his attacker. Skeeter knocked Eric's gun arm up and away to avoid being shot then threw him to the ground. Pouncing on Eric, he slashed the razor across his chest.

Eric squealed in agony. His shirt split open and a wave of blood erupted from the wound.

"Crazy bitch?" Skeeter said, snorting. "That ain't no way to speak to a lady!" Then he swung the razor down again and again as blood splashed in wide arcs and painted the room in a fresh coat of crimson.

Ray heard his brother's bloodcurdling screams echoing down the hall.

Dear God. They're in the house.

Abandoning all vigilance at the back door and windows, he charged forward to go rescue his brother.

TWENTY-SIX

REACHING DOWN THROUGH THE ATTIC hatch, Jessie furiously clawed at the wedged panels that obstructed her passage. Her fingernails bent, then snapped, and still she pounded on the doors to work them free. The sound of Eric's screaming from down below whipped her bloodlust into even more of a frenzy. She had to get down there to earn her share.

Salivating from the excitement, Skeeter drew the blade back and forth across Eric's chest, slashing his flesh into wet, crimson ribbons.

Gun still in hand, Eric swung the pistol at his attacker's face and pulled the trigger.

Skeeter ducked and barely avoided the bullet meant for him, but the blast was so close it still singed the peach fuzz on his ear and left a high-pitched ringing that only added to the lunacy already burning his fevered brain.

"Pigfucker!" Skeeter screamed, shaking his head like he had an earful of water.

Before Eric could adjust his aim and take another shot, Skeeter shoved the razor under the man's armpit and slid the blade up with all his might, slicing through nerves and muscles.

Eric unleashed a torturous howl. The gun dropped from his grasp and his arm drew into his side for protection. Skeeter held him down with one hand and started to carve around the biceps and triceps muscles on Eric's damaged arm, rendering the limb useless and handicapping him even more in the fight.

Ray skidded into the entryway near the hall and was welcomed by a thunderous boom at the front door when its window exploded in at him.

Broken glass blew in from one side and a chunk of the wall blew out from the other. Ray narrowly missed the shotgun pellets but not the debris that burst out of the sheetrock from the blast. It slammed into his face and sent him reeling back, off-balance, until he fell to the ground and smashed his head against the wood floor.

Ray lay on his side, his head spinning and lids fluttering from the grit burning his eyes. The cold, hardwood floor felt good against his hot, flushed face. He wanted to lie there for a few seconds, just long enough to catch his breath. But Eric's ghastly screams through the open doorway at the end of the hall forced him to rise.

"Help me with these goddamn doors!" Jessie screamed down at Skeeter. No matter how hard she tried, it seemed impossible to work the wedged panels loose.

Drenched in Eric's blood, Skeeter glanced over at the closet. Jessie's hands dipped just below the top of its doorframe and pounded at the collapsed panels. "Now you just hold up, baby girl!" he said. "Be with ya in a sec."

Even with the strength draining faster than the blood from his body, Eric still fought for his life. He limply swung at Skeeter's jaw but the man only had to lean back slightly to dodge the weak blow.

Skeeter laughed and licked himself then reached into an open wound in Eric's chest and pinched a strip of pectoral muscle, stretching the glistening tendon like a wet rubber band. Eric shrieked and flopped on the floor, the excruciating pain making him nearly vomit. Skeeter pulled the muscle until a small piece tore off, the rest of it snapping back into the wound. Examining it with pride, he smiled and quickly gobbled it up.

"Goddamnit!" Jessie screamed from the closet. "Let me down there!"

Skeeter knew he shouldn't be so selfish. Putting down this sow had been all his doing and he was damn proud of that fact, but now he could use Jessie's help with the other brother.

It was time to let her in and a solid kick to the bottom of the wedged doors should do just that. Still straddling Eric, Skeeter rose to his knees and dragged him closer to the closet. Like a cat carrying a dead mouse, he refused to let go of his trophy. Skeeter licked himself with excitement and scooted Eric closer, leaving a wide trail of blood across the floor. Eric groaned and his breath came out a wheezing gurgle.

"C'mon, Slick," Skeeter said in a mocking tone. "Almost there."

Eric's eyes rattled in their sockets. Half-blinded from pain, it was a battle to simply stay focused on his attacker. He coughed up blood and kicked out slightly, offering little resistance.

"C'mon! Hurry!" Jessie screamed from the closet.

"I am! Shut your damn m—"

Heavy footsteps over Skeeter's shoulder stole his final word. He swung to the open doorway and gasped like a kid caught looking at a porno mag.

Ray stood in the entrance with blood running down his face and into his eyes. His trembling gun was drawn and aimed at Skeeter. Still dazed, he blinked and looked around the room for his brother and saw some sort of a commotion happening within the closet.

Was that Eric who was trapped in there?

Wiping blood from his brow with the back of his hand, the red quivering mass Skeeter straddled slowly came into focus and Ray's eyes widened in horror.

Eric flopped his head over in Ray's direction and stared up at him, his twisted expression a mixture of agony and vulnerability.

Ray stood slack-jawed, unable to accept the realization the shredded and destroyed body lying in the giant pool of blood belonged to his brother. It sent a crippling wave of nausea over him. The scene was nearly identical to those final nightmarish moments he last saw his wife. His chest tightened, clamping so tight around his lungs, his breath rushed out. He staggered and fell against the doorframe and tried to use it for support.

Skeeter wrenched Eric's head up by his hair and pressed the razor against his outstretched neck, the violent action making Eric whimper.

"You drop that fuckin' gun," Skeeter screamed, "or I'll kill him!"

All movement in the closet quickly ceased.

The room became a vacuum, void of sound, until …

"Help me …" Eric whispered. "Please, Ray …"

Ray's eyes welled with tears.

"I said drop the fuckin' gun!" Skeeter yanked Eric's head up higher. "Or I'll slit his—"

Ray squeezed the trigger. A deafening explosion. A muzzle flash. And a chunk of Skeeter's skull blew apart. The bullet's impact snapped the man's head back with such force, it took his entire body with it. Skeeter flew off Eric and flopped to the ground like a ragdoll. After a loud gasp, he went still and was dead.

Shuffling around his brother's expanding pool of blood, Ray knelt beside Eric and tried to assess the damage.

Portions of Eric's arms and legs were carved to the bone, his chest reduced to crimson ribbons that spilled to the floor. No wound could be singled out where applying pressure would stem the massive blood flow. The man was hemorrhaging everywhere.

Ray fought to keep a brave face, his trembling hands pillowing Eric's head. "You … you're gonna be okay," he lied. "Just fine, lil' brother."

Eric glanced over at Skeeter, slumped in the corner. "Nice shot, man …" He smiled then coughed up a bloody glob that landed back on his face and in his eyes.

Ray wiped the mess away so Eric could see then gently cradled him. "You just hang in there. Try not to move."

At the backdoor, an eyeball appeared in one of the bullet holes. It glanced down at the chair wedged under the knob then scanned the room.

A key slid into the lock.

The deadbolt turned over with a faint squeak.

The door lurched forward, dislodging the obstruction, then slowly opened about six inches, sliding the chair's legs silently across the polished hardwood floor.

A thick, freckled arm coated in red hair floated in and lifted the chair out of the way. The door slowly opened and Red's shadow fell over its threshold.

TWENTY-SEVEN

"I'M GONNA GET YA OUT of here," Ray said. It was a lie. He knew Eric was dying. The blood loss was far too great. His chest had suffered massive trauma and his life was literally draining from him with each passing second.

Eric floated in and out of consciousness. He shook his head, fighting to stay awake, then weakly fumbled through his back pocket with the arm he was able to move.

"What? What are you looking for?" Ray asked. "Stay still. Save your energy."

Eric pulled out the envelope containing the directions to Oklahoma.

Ray's birthday gift.

He slapped it into Ray's hand and squeezed both tight.

"Finish it …" He coughed up more blood.

Ray glanced at the envelope, unsure of how to respond. Although his intention was never to go, he still answered, "Not without you."

Struggling to rise, Eric got in Ray's face. "No! Don't feed me that shit! You do it, goddamn it!'"

"I will. I will. Just-just relax, okay?"

"Promise … promise me … you'll get him. Make him talk. Give up who hired him. Then kill 'em all. Promise me that."

Ray nodded slightly. He already knew Eric's screams were going to haunt him for years to come. Would it really cause any more sleeplessness if he added a few more screams to that choir?

"You promise, Ray! Don't … don't make this all for nothing! For God's sake, fuckin' promise me that! Please!!"

Ray locked eyes with Eric. What was being asked of him was suicidal. And at that moment of madness, the answer never seemed so simple. He nodded. "I promise."

Eric smiled and a long strand of bloody drool stretched from his lower lip. "Good. Now use these inbred fuckers for what they are … *practice*." Hissing between clenched teeth, his back arched then he slowly sank to the ground. His body deflated with an escaping groan that slowly faded to silence. Eric went still, his eyes glazed over while staring up at his older brother.

Ray shook him slightly. Eric gave no response. He moved him again and whispered, "Eric …?"

Nothing.

Ray's eyes filled with tears. His breathing became hitched. He eased Eric's head back to the ground and held down his lids until they remained closed then wiped the blood-matted hair off his dead brother's forehead.

All he had left in this life was now gone.

Erased.

He accepted all blame for Rachel's death and that was something he'd gladly continue torturing himself over until his dying day. But, Eric? No. They'd simply stumbled across the wrong people at the wrong time when they hitched that ride. These people were predators. Killers. Monsters. And once he erased their bloodline—as his own now was—he'd finish the job Eric set out to do.

Happy Birthday, Ray.

Thank you, Eric. Thank you for the gift.

Leaning over the body, he snatched up Eric's gun and shoved the bloody envelope into his pants pocket. He reloaded both pistols and tossed the spent casings to the ground where they landed in the pool of blood. After the last bullet was loaded, he snapped the revolver's cylinder shut with a flick of the wrist.

Standing in the middle of the room, Ray bowed his head and closed his eyes, sealing the flow of tears shed for his brother. He stood frozen. Listened to the house's silence.

Then, from out of that void ...

A creak from above. In the ceiling.

Ray's eyes snapped open. Both barrels swung up. He waited for something more.

The wood groaned above. To the left.

Another creak. This time just over the bed.

He adjusted his aim accordingly then fired both guns. Chunks of the ceiling's popcorn texture blew apart and rained like snowfall. Ray continued firing, expanding his aim a foot from the last bullet hole for maximum coverage. Maximum damage.

A loud thud from above and the ceiling bowed and cracked. Ray put two bullets in the bulging mass. Then the ceiling exploded, vomiting drywall, chunks of pink insulation, and a woman's body.

Falling, Jessie clipped the corner of the bed and catapulted back up, smashing against the wall. She landed in the foot-wide gap between it and the mattress set.

Ray stuck one of the guns in his waistband and grabbed hold of the footboard to rip the bed away from the wall and make sure the threat was eliminated.

Pulling the bed toward him, a bloody arm shot up from the other side. Ray jumped back and raised his pistol as Jessie slowly rose, using the wall for support and smearing its surface with a fresh coat of blood.

Hunched over and coughing bloody phlegm, she seeped from gunshot wounds to the chest and leg. One arm was dislocated from the fall and hung limply at her side. The butcher's knife dropped from her grasp and landed by Eric's corpse.

Ray drew a bead on her and stepped back as she slowly advanced.

Her breath now a moist wheeze, she glared defiantly at him and limped closer. "We'll get ya, fucker." She laughed maniacally then screamed, "Just like we got your brother! Made 'em squeal real good like a fuckin' p—!"

Ray silenced her with a single shot. The bullet punched through Jessie's forehead and exited the other side. Blood and gray matter splattered the hanging bedsheet behind her then the window shattered. The impact from the gunshot sent her stumbling back. Her legs caught the edge of the sill and her body flipped over and out the broken window, disappearing into the beautiful, bright sunlight.

Lew had just made it to the window outside the slaughter room when he heard the multiple gunshots coming from inside. He dropped to his belly and rolled over, pressing himself as tight against the house as possible to avoid detection. He remained there until the window above him shattered and Jessie's body flipped out. Her corpse hit the hard ground with a loud slap then lay frozen. Twisted.

Lew scrambled to his knees and hid behind a rusted fifty-five-gallon drum leaning against the house.

Things were getting *way* out of hand now. It was time for Plan B.

Glancing from the shattered window to Jessie's body and back again, Lew kept the shotgun trained on the opening and continued his retreat until safely disappearing around the corner.

With head cocked and eyes glazed, Ray stood rooted in front of the shattered window and admired the vibrant colors of the flower garden in the distance outside.

How could there be such beauty among all this evil?

Then his lids fluttered and vision racked into focus. It was time to kill whoever he'd been fending off at the living room window. If they'd wanted in so badly, now he'd be more than happy to open the door and bid them welcome.

Using the final three bullets in his pocket, Ray reloaded his pistol and stepped into the hall ... where Red stood at the end of the corridor with sawed-off shotgun in hand.

Both men seemed surprised at the sight of the other. Red drew first. Ray jumped back into the room and the door frame exploded behind him. He shook off the debris then crouched to scan outside the room.

At the end of the hall, Red retreated for cover, disappearing around the corner and into the kitchen.

Ray squeezed off two shots that missed their target.

In response, Red reappeared and unleashed the remaining barrel of his sawed-off.

The wall closest to Ray blew apart. He jumped back for cover then returned fire in the smoky hall before his hammer fell on an empty chamber.

In the kitchen, Red snapped open the sawed-off and dropped its smoking shells to the floor. When he heard Ray's gun click empty and the man curse, a big grin stretched across his freckled face. It sounded like the son-of-a-bitch had just run out of ammo.

Ray dropped his gun and pulled Eric's pistol from the back of his waistband. Pushing open the cylinder, he emptied it into his hand to see how many shots he had left.

All were hollow brass. He set the empty gun down beside him and sighed deeply.

Red dropped two shells into his gun and snapped the barrel shut. With head bobbing and cheeks puffing, he psyched himself up to go in for the kill. "Oh, yeah!" he bellowed. Then peeled off the wall and whipped around the corner, into the hall.

Ray was already there with teeth bared. Colliding with Red, he grabbed the shotgun's barrel and pushed it up at the ceiling. Both men fought for control of the gun. Ray threw an elbow into Red's face, stunning him briefly. Before he could take advantage of the strike, half of the kitchen chair beside them blew apart and flipped over.

Both Ray and Red paused long enough to look up at the tip of the shotgun then at each other, questioning how a barrel aimed at the ceiling could've shot the chair on the floor.

A shotgun racked over their shoulders.

"Get outta the fuckin' way, ya shaved ape!"

The men spun in the direction of the voice and saw Lew standing outside one of the living room windows. He was pointing his shotgun in at them, waving its smoking barrel, yelling at Red to move.

Ray spun Red around and used the beefy man as a shield. He prayed the old bastard wasn't crazy enough to shoot through one of his own to get to him.

From the panicked look on his face, Red must've had the same thought. "Don't you shoot me!" he screamed over his shoulder to Lew. "I got this!"

Ray jerked the barrel away from Red, extending the man's arms, then used the slack to immediately slam the shotgun back into his face. It was a solid shot that snapped his head back with a sickening crack, but Red still held on.

Ray slid his finger over the ones Red had guarding the dual triggers. The shotgun whipped around and its aim fell on Lew at the window.

The old man's eyes widened.

Ray pushed down on Red's fingers, depressing a trigger and unleashing one of the barrels.

The blast shredded the curtains above Lew's head and clipped the window frame, raining splinters down upon his bald pate. He shrieked and jumped back from the opening. Falling on his ass, he wiped his head and his palm came away red.

"Ah, hell!" He wheeled around and looked at the old garage. "Enough of this shit! It's definitely time now!"

Ray tangled a leg around one of Red's and shoved the man with all his might. Thrown off balance, Red fell into the living room, but took Ray with him.

Both slammed onto the hardwood floor and lost their grip on the shotgun, slick with sweat and blood. The weapon slid across the ground—out of reach—and came to a stop just beyond the couch.

Scrambling to his feet, Red was first to rush for the gun. Ray sprung up and tackled him. Colliding with such force, they flew over the sofa and crashed into the strip of wall between the two shattered windows. The sheetrock crumpled upon impact and spit them back onto the glass-strewn floor.

Razor shards dug into their flesh, causing both men to hiss in pain. Fresh wounds spilled forth warm blood. Trying to retrieve the shotgun became a battle of endurance as both men raced over the glass on hands and knees. The thin flesh covering their joints shredded. Glass grinded against bone. And a slick trail of blood painted the floor red.

Red took the lead and kicked back, his foot catching Ray on the shoulder. The blow shoved him backwards over the broken glass, the pain rivaling that of sliding down a cheese grater. Ray screamed in agony and rolled sideways, slamming into the cinderblock thrown through the window earlier. He went to push the piece of cement out of his way, then paused.

Finally reaching the gun, Red snatched it up and whipped around for the kill. Before he could raise the sawed-off and take aim, his eyes bulged as a large object hurled toward his face.

The cinderblock made a direct hit. Upon impact, his head snapped to the side and he crumpled to the floor.

Ray scuttled forward and closed the distance, springing on top of the prone man and grabbing the gun.

Dazed and bloody, with his eye swelling shut and face scraped raw, Red kept his grip on the shotgun and stayed in the fight. But Ray overpowered him, wrenching the gun around and plugging both of its sawed-off barrels under the man's chin.

Red screamed and fought to protect the trigger, cupping its guard, knowing he was definitely on the wrong end of the gun.

Using his body weight and one hand to pin down the sawed-off, Ray pummeled Red with blows, hoping the man would release the trigger guard to block his assault.

Red absorbed each punch since priority number one was getting the goddamn muzzle out from under his jaw … and in his weakened state, he needed both hands on the gun to accomplish that.

Ray managed to pry loose one of Red's beefy digits protecting the guard. He took a firm hold of the finger and snapped it at the second joint.

Red squealed in pain.

Ray wiggled his own finger into the guard but Red squeezed tighter to prevent him from discharging the gun. The problem was, in his haste, Red clamped down *too* hard … and pulled the trigger himself.

In the split second before Red blew apart his own head, both men locked eyes. One in defeat. The other, victory. Then Ray winced at the explosion that ended with a reverb of a wet splat.

When all went still, he collapsed off the faceless man and pried the sawed-off from his rigid grasp. With both barrels empty—and now useless—Ray dropped it and fought for air. Every muscle in his body was taut and on fire. With the adrenaline of the moment already fading, he began to feel glass scraping against bone and the burning of shredded flesh. Then the large shard of glass protruding from his outer thigh caught his eye. Knowing he better act fast, Ray ripped it out and the bolt of pain that shot through his leg made him let off an ungodly howl.

Dragging the body wrapped in a dirty tarp closer to the garage door, Lew froze when he heard the shotgun blast. The old man craned his neck around the corner, looking back toward the house. Was the city boy dead? He eyed the cattle prod balancing on the tarp then the padlocked door over his shoulder.

Maybe there wasn't the need to kick the hornet's nest now.

He waited for a sign all was clear. That the deed was done. Instead, Lew heard Ray's scream echoing from the house when the man pulled the shard of glass from his leg.

Lew stood planted, unsure if the sound was a delayed reaction from being on the receiving end of the shotgun blast or some battle cry of victory. He alternated glances from the bulky tarp to the cattle prod, then back at the garage door.

"Awe … fuck it." He dragged the tarp closer to the entrance.

The time to play it safe had long since passed.

TWENTY-EIGHT

A **RIPPED-UP ARMCHAIR COVER USED AS** a makeshift tourniquet stemmed the blood flow at Ray's thigh. Fighting back the pain, he gingerly crouched beside Red's corpse to check the man's pockets for more shotgun shells or a set of keys.

Neither was found.

He exhaled in defeat and slowly rose, wincing loudly. Keys or no keys, it was time to leave. Now.

Ray limped out of the living room and disappeared into the hallway.

Standing in the open doorway of the garage, Lew peered into the void that swallowed his outstretched shadow. Even with a barn door open, most of the interior remained cloaked in darkness. Stacked piles of junk and discarded debris formed shadowy walkways like a haunted house maze during Halloween. The shaft of light through the open door only traveled far enough to illuminate a rusted refrigerator, rotten piles of lumber, and an old, rusted car frame picked clean of its parts.

"Precious?" Lew stared at his immediate corner, nearly black as a moonless night. The last thing needed right now was some sneak attack by the giant. He aimed the cattle prod at the corner and pressed the trigger, using its electrical current for light. The crackling bolt at its tip blasted away the darkness and made the shadows dance in a blue tint. Only a rotting stack of fence posts stood there.

Sighing in relief, Lew turned and faced the rest of the garage. "Got something for ya." He returned to the bulky tarp and dragged it deeper inside, making sure it stayed within the shaft of light. Lew wiped his bald head and looked at the bloody sweat greasing his palm.

A groan sounded from the darkness.

Lew whipped around and pointed the prod in its direction.

"Get out here, boy!" Electricity crackled and its blue glow lit the immediate area.

A whimper came from somewhere ahead.

"I said ... Get. Your ass. Out here."

Heavy steps approached from the shadows. Lew swallowed hard, gripped the prod tight, and hoped he wasn't making one hell of a mistake.

Steeling himself, Ray knelt over his brother's corpse to search for more ammunition. His trembling hands hovered over the mangled body then pulled back, afraid to touch it.

There's no time for this, he thought, *so just do it.*

Almost like plunging into an ice bath, Ray took a deep breath then leaned over and quickly patted down Eric for any bullets. When none were found, he shuffled away and wiped Eric's blood off on his pants.

Without ammo, the guns were useless. But he needed a weapon. Something. Anything. Skeeter's straight razor lay on the ground, its blade still open and covered with Eric's coagulating blood. Ray kicked it away. There was no way he'd touch that damn thing.

Jessie's butcher's knife lay by the window amid the broken glass. Ray snatched it up then found a clean sheet in the corner and used it to cover Eric. As the fabric fell and gently molded to the contours of his corpse, the white sheet instantly turned red from absorbing the massive amount of blood.

After doing a quick search and finding nothing of importance in Skeeter's pockets, Ray stood in the doorway and stared at his brother's shrouded corpse then slowly turned and left the room.

His eyes narrowing, Lew waited for his vision to adjust to the darkness. Outlines of familiar items materialized then the shape he'd been waiting for came into view. It was humongous, standing in a hunched position. Cowering.

"Get out here, boy. Ya got work to do."

Electricity danced at the tip of the cattle prod. The large, shadowy figure whimpered and shook its head.

"Precious! I'm warnin' ya!"

When Precious didn't move, Lew lunged forward and jabbed the prod into the behemoth's ribcage and lit him up. Precious screamed and lurched away, shuffling down the wall and swiping a rusted refrigerator out of his way like it was an empty cardboard box.

The old man followed him with more threats. "That's right, boy! You want more of this? Then move your fat ass!" Lew wiped his brow and saw the blood on his hand. He held it up for Precious. "See! See what them city folks did?"

Precious froze. His whimpering ceased.

Lew puffed up, knowing his taunts were working. "That's right. City folk. They hurt me! *Me!*"

The shadowy figure stood erect and towered over the old man. He grunted and stepped forward and Lew backpedaled. Precious slowly advanced, his arms waving, asking for Lew's bloody hand. Lew quickly withdrew it and Precious halted.

Only the good little boys and girls taste the sweetness.

Precious waited patiently for permission but when it didn't happen fast enough, he whined like a dog teased with a biscuit.

Lew drew out the moment, loving the control he had over the beast, before finally yielding his bloody hand. "Okay. But if you bite me, I'll zap your fat, fuckin' ass!"

Two gigantic hands lunged out of the darkness and clamped around Lew's wrist. The old man resisted slightly but stayed put and made damn sure his other hand was ready with the cattle prod if things went awry. Precious leaned closer, into the strip of sunlight blasting through the open door. He pulled the bloody hand up, allowing only his mouth and nose to be illuminated. The chapped lips below the cleft palate peeled back and unsheathed a row of crooked, jagged teeth. Like a giant, pink slug, his tongue flopped out and lapped at the blood, leaving thick ribbons of drool stretching between maw and hand.

Lew grimaced and turned away. *Just let him get the taste*, he thought. *So the real fun can begin.*

TWENTY-NINE

THE BACKDOOR INCHED OPEN. RAY peeked out and saw it was a straight shot to Pork Chop's Jeep parked about fifteen yards away. The keys had to be in its ignition since they weren't found on the man's body.

Instead of rushing outside to get his head blown off by someone lying in wait, Ray threw open the door, ducked back inside, and waited for all hell to break loose by way of gunfire. Or at least for someone to pop off a premature round.

But there were no shots. No exploding walls or doors. No bloodthirsty lunatics charging for an attack. According to his count, the only threats left were the old man and whatever Eric had shot at inside the garage. That is, unless Lew had called for reinforcements, in which Pork Chop might have been a part of that new wave. He had to proceed like there were more out there waiting.

Clutching Jessie's butcher knife, Ray slowly rose and looked outside again. The place appeared deserted, which made his stomach twist in a knot of dread. Was he stepping into a trap? Knowing he had to move, he quickly swallowed that fear and scoped out his path. Splitting the distance between him and the Jeep was a small pile of rusted, fifty-five-gallon drums that could be used for cover if things went awry.

There you go. Now, move! his brain commanded his feet. Ray limped out of the house with butcher knife in hand. Once off the porch, his injured leg buckled a few steps across the uneven ground. He stumbled forward but managed to steady himself and push on.

He made the Jeep his main focus. Not the stabbing pain in his leg. Or stopping to catch his breath. He limped past the drums, his head whipping back and forth scanning for movement.

Finally making it to the Jeep, he ripped open the driver's door, reached around the steering column, and prayed to hear the jingle of keys.

The ignition was empty. Ray punched the seat in frustration.

They had to be there somewhere. Clipped to the visor. In the console. Or the glovebox. Under the seat. Somewhere.

When nothing was found, Ray forced himself to abandon the vehicle and move on to search Jessie's red pickup parked near the old wooden garage.

His hand licked clean and glistening with saliva, Lew yanked his arm free of Precious's grasp and wiped it on his shirt in disgust. "Goddamn. Drooling like a big fuckin' baby!"

Precious stepped forward, hungry for more.

"No! That's enough!" The man shoved the cattle prod in the giant's gut and pressed the trigger.

Precious howled in pain and scuttled back into the shadows.

The unholy scream pulled Ray from the pickup's floorboard. He slid out from Jessie's truck and moved down its body, taking cover behind the rear tire. Whoever made the cry was inside the garage, just on the other side of the vehicle. And like Eric's warning, they sounded very large and pissed off. He peeked over the bed. The wall of the garage facing him had no windows. But he remembered seeing one on the opposite side.

Don't do it. Just get outta here.

Like a gambling addict trying to walk away from the table … *But what if this is the one? What if there's a car inside?*

His gut squirmed and his scalp prickled, telling him he was being dealt a very bad hand. But he knew he had to check it out.

A peek. Just a peek. Just to rule it out.

It took a moment to work up the courage but he did eventually move forward. Toward the garage.

"Enough of this horseshit! Ya gotta job to do!" Lew shocked Precious again and hooted. He shuffled back and stared at the giant's crotch.

"Christ almighty! You piss yourself?"

Precious covered his urine-soaked lap with his huge, grimy hands. The onslaught of shocks from the cattle prod had made him lose control of his bladder muscles.

Lew jabbed him in the chest with the tool. "No! Don't you touch yourself, boy! Move them hands."

Precious slowly did as he was told. Lew pointed to the house. "Now, listen up, fuckface. They're in there right now. Gettin' all up in our business." The cattle prod dropped a few inches to Precious's waist. The giant shook his head, *No more.* Lew ignored him. "Inside. Our. Home. You hearin' me?!" The old man looked at the urine soaked pants. "Goddammit! While you were out here hidin' like some chickenshit, they killed your brothers! They're all dead!" He pinned the tip of the prod in Precious's crotch, ensuring it made direct contact with the wet spot for maximum conductivity. "They're all dead because of you! You! Ya piece of shit!" He pressed the button and sent bolts of electricity swarming into the giant's crotch like angry bees. Precious wailed. His knees unhinged and he crashed to the ground.

Ray heard the bloodcurdling cries and stood frozen against the side of the garage. He white-knuckled the knife handle. *Fuck this. Just run, Stupid!* his brain screamed. *You don't even wanna know what's going on in there.* He stared at the butcher knife in his left hand, sizing it up, knowing—based on the sound of the thing inside—it might as well be a plastic spork he was holding.

But then his eyes fell on his wedding band. Caked in blood.

The clock was ticking.

He'd never make it to the meeting if he just ran and hid in the woods like some frightened animal. And then the living hell he and Eric had been through for the past twenty-four hours would've been for nothing.

No. Running wasn't an option. He wouldn't have Eric's death be in vain. He had a job to do. A mission. And to accomplish it, he'd need a vehicle.

Taking a deep breath, Ray pushed off the wall and moved for the garage's entrance.

The old man shocked Precious again, but this time showed mercy by raising the prod's tip from balls to belly. "Oh, it gets better! So much better!" he said. "Check this out." He rushed back to the tarp. "Looky-here. C'mere, buddy. C'mere-c'mere-c'mere. I ain't gonna shock ya none. Promise. Now, c'mon."

Precious cautiously approached.

Peeling back the cloth, Lew reached in and grabbed a handful of bloody locks then wrenched Jessie up by her hair, out of the tarp, like pulling a rabbit from a top hat. "Looky-here! Looky at what they did to your Jessie-Jess!" He danced a quick jig, kicking up a cloud of dust, then pulled her head back to make sure her face was clearly visible.

Precious stepped closer. He grunted and shook his head, unable to process the spectacle.

"She's dead, ya dumb fuck!" Lew said. "D-E-D ... dead! They killed her!"

Precious shifted his gaze from Jessie's gore-soaked face to Lew and back again. A spark of understanding ignited. The giant groaned.

"That's right! They killed your Jessie-Jess!"

Precious lunged forward, reaching for her body, but was met by the crackling end of the cattle prod. He reeled back into the shadows.

"Nuh-uh! You don't touch her until you do your job. And that job is to get the fuckers that did this! You get 'em and you tear 'em to pieces." Still holding her by her bloody mane, Lew swayed Jessie's upper body back and forth like some grotesque marionette. "You get those shits that did *this* to your Jessie."

Precious howled and slapped his head.

The old man grinned. "That's right, boy. Work it up!"

Precious punched himself, slamming his beefy mitts against his forehead.

"Harder!"

The behemoth hit himself again. And again. Each strike more vicious.

Lew continued his jig while swaying Jessie around like a cobra dancing for a snake charmer. "That's right! Ya should've been there for her! She was *always* there for you! And when she needed ya the most, you failed her! *This* ..."—he pointed to the bullet hole in her forehead—"is all your fault!"

Precious screamed and pummeled himself. He flailed wildly, smashing into the surrounding debris and knocking the junk over.

"That's right, boy! Harder!" Lew lunged forward like a fencer and jabbed the prod into Precious's gut, shocking the beast into even more of a frenzy. "Said *harder!*"

Through the open doorway, Ray watched the freak show taking place inside. Whoever the old man was shocking with the prod was cloaked in the shadows. But it was plain to see the guy was big. A giant. And someone not to be messed with.

Seeing Jessie's corpse, the realization he failed to even search her body for any keys was like a punch to the gut.

But it was obviously too late to do anything about it now.

Lew shocked Precious again then wrenched Jessie's head from side to side to punctuate each one of his words. "They. Killed. Her. Now she's gone. Forever!" All that movement bounced the woman's large breasts. Lew did a double take at her cleavage, all slick with blood. It was glistening. Lubed up. Lew curled his upper lip and groaned. Then he wiggled her some more. "Of course …"

Precious stopped his antics and watched the old man ogle his Jessie.

Lew placed the cattle prod on the ground to free up a hand then cupped one of her breasts.

The giant grunted, but the sound trailed off into a low growl. A warning.

"Of course …" The man gave her tit a squeeze and pinched the hardened nipple through the fabric. "The bitch still might have some use before she stinks to high heaven." Licking his lips, he slid a hand down the front of her tank top and groped bare flesh. "Ya know, as long as ya get to her before she sets up. Just takes a little spit is all. Spit and—"

The beast sprung from the shadows. Before Lew could raise an arm to defend himself, Precious clamped both hands around the man's head. A savage twist. A loud crack. And the old man's skull spun around one hundred and eighty degrees, flinging blood-tinged saliva from his gaping mouth across the dirt behind him.

When his head came to a stop, it faced Ray. They locked eyes and a look of recognition washed over Lew's face. Ray's heart leaped to his throat, expecting the old man to call out and give his position away.

But Lew didn't shout. Only let off a death rattle, gurgling air worked its way out of his crushed and twisted windpipe.

Ray quickly pulled back around the corner and raised the butcher knife, poised for an attack. His heart hammering double-time, he waited, dreading the sound of approaching footsteps.

The only noise that followed was the thud of Lew's body hitting the dirt and the cries of a wounded animal—guttural wails that quickly turned to a hitching sob. The crying grew faint as it traveled deeper into the garage.

Wanting absolutely zero to do with the thing inside, Ray figured it was time to cut his losses and just get his ass out of there. He could backtrack to the small road they first spotted Jessie's house from, travel it up a way, and take a chance on coming across another place—hopefully one where the owners weren't related to these psychopaths.

Ray made his move, circling back to avoid detection. About to duck past the shattered window, his feet crunched the broken glass littering the ground.

The breath froze in his lungs. He slid back against the wall beside the window for cover and winced at his carelessness. He waited, listening to see if he'd given himself away.

Dead silence.

Then a huge arm erupted from the window opening. It swung at Ray, who jumped back and narrowly escaped the blow. The massive hand slammed against the garage and raked its siding, clawing five jagged grooves down the wood surface.

As fast as the arm appeared, it retracted into the darkness. A mighty roar sounded and all hell broke loose inside like the whole place was getting turned upside down.

Ray, now filled with an absolute terror that overrode any stabbing pain in his leg, broke into a mad dash across the field toward the woods. By the time he hit the treeline, he heard the second set of garage doors burst open behind him. He threw a quick glance over his shoulder and saw the hulking form give chase across the field. Ray spun back around and barreled into the woods with his injured leg dragging, leaving a trail in the dead foliage.

A trail that could be easily tracked.

THIRTY

SWATTING AWAY BRANCHES THAT BLOCKED his path, Ray fled deeper into the woods, frantically searching for a place to hide. His heart drummed in his chest. He gasped for breath.

About a hundred yards in, the woods spit him out into a field of waist-high grass. Unable to see the ground, he moved cautiously across the uneven terrain to avoid twisting an ankle or buckling a knee. As the landscape began to incline, both legs quickly turned to jelly and a fire ignited throughout his muscles. Continuing his ascent, the horizon vanished and was replaced by blue sky over swaying reeds. Ray raked the grass out of his way to clear a path and pushed on.

Without warning, the ground abruptly ended and his eyes exploded in their sockets. He gasped and skidded to a halt, teetering at the edge of the drop. His boots kicked up a wave of dirt that crashed into the creek twenty feet below. Ray scuttled back and ducked for cover, collapsing on all fours with a stabbing stitch in his side that seemed hell-bent on crippling him.

While trying to catch his breath, he took in his surroundings.

Maybe the location was a good place to hide with the small cliff being one less entry point he'd have to worry about. Then again, it also trapped him if an attack came from the rear. No, it was best to move on.

Crawling forward on his belly to remain out of sight, he peered over the cliff's edge to seek a safe passage down.

The face of the drop curved back underneath him and offered no slope to slide down. The water in the creek bed below was stagnant and swampy, making it damn near impossible to determine its depth. A few rocks broke the water's surface and were spaced close enough to use as stepping stones to get across if he were able to make it down there. The shore on the opposite side led to a gradual incline that continued into the next thicket of trees, a place much better suited to hide.

The sharp crack of a branch in the distance spun Ray around. Gripping the butcher knife tight, he slowly rose out of the grass and looked across the field.

Precious stood at the base of the far treeline. The hulking figure was aimed in his direction. Ray dropped to the ground but suspected he'd already been spotted. When the animalistic scream echoed toward him—confirming his suspicion—he knew it was time to move. Now.

The quickest way down was to blindly leap into the creek below and pray its murky water was more than a few inches deep. If it wasn't, he'd break a leg and forfeit any chance of escape. No. Jumping was far too risky. He slid closer to the edge and saw the cliff face twenty yards to his left had enough outward slope to slide down. He hobbled for it.

Heavy steps approached in the distance.

Precious raced through the field, homing in on his prey.

Ray reached the steep face and slid down the embankment, sending up a dust cloud and an avalanche of dirt clogs in his wake. He grabbed at the wispy roots poking out of the earth as a means to slow his descent and maintain balance.

Finally reaching the creek, he leaped for a rock breaking the surface. The slick algae coating the stone caused his foot to slip and he plunged into the water. Before he had a chance to hold his breath, Ray hit bottom and discovered the creek was only knee deep. It took a moment to process he wouldn't need to swim his way out.

Ray trudged the fifteen feet to the other side. Completely gassed, he stumbled and collapsed onto the muddy shore, stabbing the butcher knife into the dirt. The fight slowly drained from his exhausted body until he glanced over at his hand clawing the muddy ground and caught the gold reflection of his wedding band—now a constant reminder there was more on his plate for today than just survival. Lying there, gasping for air, he forced himself to rise, snatched up the blade, and continued on up the opposite embankment.

Entering the woods, Ray weaved between the trees, bouncing off some and using others for support. His overheated brain told him to climb one and hide, but his fatigued body lacked the strength needed to pull himself up high enough to avoid detection.

A thunderous splash came from over his shoulder.

He spun back to the creek and movement caught his eye.

A large, misshapen head with long patchy hair rose from the horizon as his pursuer climbed out of the creek bed.

Ray sized up his options. Run a few more torturous feet and risk being spotted … or hide? If he let the son-of-a-bitch plow past him, maybe he could backtrack to the garage and check Jessie's body for the truck keys. Sure, by now it was beating a dead horse but he had to rule out the possibility, especially since he was clueless as to if there was even another house with a vehicle further up the road.

So hide it was. He slid behind a large oak, putting its trunk between him and his pursuer. Ray tightly clutched the butcher knife and sucked in deep breaths. Any approaching footsteps were muted by the thunderous pulse in his ears. If he couldn't control his gasping, it'd surely give him away. His nerves vibrated, making him tremble.

Just relax, he told himself. Slower ... more drawn out ... breaths. He slowly inhaled. Exhaled. *That's it. Calm down.*

Then from the other side of the oak ...

A branch snapped.

Ray's gut dropped. He stood frozen, terrified to move. His mind raced. Dear God, had he been spotted? Or maybe that thing was only catching its breath, standing there, scanning the distance for any sign of him. He pressed tighter against the tree and remained still.

While Ray cowered behind the oak, Precious crept closer. He knew Ray's exact location. Not only was it the tracks left by dragging an injured leg across the ground that gave him away, but the oh-so-sweet smell of the city man's fear. Normally, the fragrance would rumble his belly and stir his loins, but not this time. Oh, no. This time it was fueling a rage. A need to bring pain and suffering. Because this tiny, wounded thing hiding on the opposite side of the tree had killed his Jessie.

And Precious planned to paint the woods red with its blood.

THIRTY-ONE

HIS BACK FLUSH WITH THE tree, Ray clenched the knife so hard his hand trembled. His eyes swam in their sockets, waiting to catch movement in his periphery so he could plunge the blade into a target.

There was a crunch of gravel to his right.

Ray ticked his head in its direction and raised the blade. He knew he had to wait until the giant appeared and was within striking distance. As kids, his father taught Eric and him to always hit first and hit hard when it came to fights. If confrontation was inevitable, don't stand there and wait to get punched—*strike first, dammit!* Ray waited, the seconds became maddening. His heart beat a mad rhythm.

The snap of another tree branch. Closer. Just opposite the trunk. This was it.

Ray rushed out from behind the tree and was immediately met with a blow to the face. The strike was like getting hit by a sledgehammer, its raw force violently snapping his head to the side. Fireworks blinded his vision and he stumbled back on rubbery legs. The shock wave from the punch caused his fingers to go numb and the knife fell from his grasp. His knees buckled and he dropped to the ground.

Ray sat on his ass, temporarily dazed and completely vulnerable. The large, cold shadow moving over him became a quick reminder of the mortal danger he was in. He snapped out of it, pushed up into a crab walk but only managed to retreat a few feet before his sluggish arms gave out. Collapsing onto his back, Ray flipped over and belly crawled, too weak and damaged to rise to his bloody knees.

A giant hand clamped over his nape, wrenched him up, and spun him around for a proper face-to-face introduction.

Held at arm's length, Ray was finally able to focus on the beast of a man pursuing him. There were no more shadows or distance to conceal the deformed and scarred features. The horror was finally brought into the light … up close and personal.

The wisps of hair, so blond it almost appeared white, blew around the malformed head like a crown of albino snakes. The skull bulged on one side like a water balloon squeezed tight and ready to burst. The eyes—buried in deep sockets under a Neanderthal brow—weren't symmetrical. A milky cataract orb like an old gray marble drooped lower than the opposite solid black eye. The nose was pressed flat against the wide face and bubbled with snot. The cleft palate bisected the upper lip, revealing rotten greenish teeth embedded in puffy, black gums. Scars and burns lined the porous flesh which was heavily dimpled like an orange peel.

Frothing with rage, Precious throttled Ray with a single hand. Holding his prey a foot off the ground, he pulled Ray closer for inspection.

As the hot, wretched breath blew against his face, Ray clung to Precious's thick forearm to relieve the pressure strangling him like a hangman's noose. He kicked wildly, hoping to catch the giant in the knee or crotch. In response, Precious simply extended his arm, temporarily moving Ray out of striking distance.

With the very life being squeezed out of him singlehandedly, Ray opened his mouth to scream but nothing sounded. The lack of oxygen caused floaters to cloud his vision like a swarm of gnats. A darkness ebbed around the edges of his field of view.

Precious drew him closer again, wanting to witness the choking panic on the man's face.

Before the shadows could swallow him whole, Ray hooked an arm back over Precious's to free up a hand. He shifted his body and rained blows at the giant's head.

The first strike only grazed Precious's cheek and did nothing.

The second one caught him on the jaw. His head snapped to the side and his grip loosened temporarily—long enough to allow Ray a gulp of air and the energy to strike again.

The next blow hammered the giant's temple. Precious grunted. His lids fluttered.

In response to the shot, Precious lunged forward and slammed his deformed head against Ray's skull, knocking the man limp before throwing him back.

Ray soared through the air and crashed to the hard earth.

Precious, not expecting the headbutt to daze him also, stumbled and tried to shake off the stars dancing around his fevered brain.

Ray fought to rise, but his aching muscles gave out, sending him face down into the dirt. As he lay there beaten and exhausted with lids half closed, a glint of light on the ground caught his attention.

It was sunlight gleaming off the butcher knife's polished blade. He focused on it and quickly realized the weapon wasn't too far out of reach. Refusing to surrender, Ray crawled for the knife.

Before he could reach it, Precious rushed him. A swift kick to the gut lifted Ray off the ground and flipped him onto his back. He hit the hard ground, groaning. His diaphragm felt like it had collapsed against his spine. Precious grabbed a handful of hair and wrenched him to his feet.

The giant swung and struck Ray in the ribs. There was a crack and an explosion of pain that caused him to grit his teeth and nearly bite off his tongue. Another blow caught Ray on the face. His knees gave out but he remained upright thanks to the firm grip Precious still had on his matted hair. The next punch to the gut landed with such force his feet swung backwards—off the ground. On the return, Precious yanked him closer and locked Ray in a bear hug, his two huge arms sealed under the man's armpits.

As Precious began to crush him, something primeval erupted from Ray. He shrieked and threw both hands over his attacker's scarred visage, searching for soft flesh to tear.

His fingers found the prize, working two tips into Precious's good eye and stretching the lid back. Precious squealed as the digits dug deep, sinking to the second joint. Tears and blood squeezed out of the pressurized socket and Ray hooked his fingers behind the giant's black orb. A violent wrench and he scooped the eyeball free, stretching the ocular tendons until they snapped. The bloody orb fell to the ground with a wet splat.

Shrieking in agony, Precious hurled the threat away.

Ray hit the ground and tumbled, a ragdoll of rubbery limbs. While Precious smacked his face to end the burning, Ray sought the knife on the ground. Disoriented, he crawled in the opposite direction then realized his mistake. He quickly backtracked, ignoring the pain from the sharp sticks and rocks that dug into his bloody palms and knees.

Cradling his damaged face, Precious caught sight of Ray through the milky haze of his cataract eye. He advanced toward his target, roaring with snot ribbons swaying from his nose. Because of his limited sight and disorientation, he zig-zagged across the uneven ground and stepped on his own severed eyeball. The orb let off a gelatinous pop and smeared across a rock. He slipped on the grue and a knee buckled, causing him to stumble and crash to the ground on all fours.

Ray seized the moment and snatched up the knife.

Precious fought to regain his bearings then slowly rose to his feet. When he moved to attack Ray, the man wasn't there. Precious squinted and a stream of blood squirted out of his raw, empty socket. He scanned the area in front of him.

Then heavy breathing came from over his shoulder.

Precious spun and Ray met him with butcher knife in hand. The blade sliced the air and Ray drove the knife deep into the giant's chest. It pierced his breast bone with a muffled thud like the stabbing of a ripe melon. Ray hit the handle with an open palm strike, burying it hilt deep into Precious's chest.

His body going erect, the giant screamed to the heavens.

Ray dropped to the ground and kicked with all his might. The heel of his boot caught Precious in the kneecap and the giant's leg collapsed inward with a loud crack of broken cartilage. Precious fell forward, his arms pinwheeling at his side in an attempt to grab hold of something—anything—to stop his fall.

Ray rolled out of the way and the behemoth belly flopped onto the knife, driving the blade even deeper into his chest.

Gasping and spitting blood, Precious writhed in agony. He flipped onto his back and clawed at the wood nub—all that was left exposed of the knife handle—that stuck out of his chest. As he flailed like a live bug pinned on a display board, a shadow fell over his prone body.

Ray stood over him with a large rock in both hands. Chest heaving and arms trembling, he struggled to remain balanced while hoisting the heavy stone over his head.

But Precious attacked first, lashing out and gripping Ray's ankle. Sharp nails tore into his flesh. Blood spurted. Ray screamed and crumpled, but used that momentum to bring the rock slamming down upon his opponent's head. A loud crack of bone and the stone bounced off the malformed skull.

Precious loosened his grip.

Ray brought the rock down again with another sickening thud then raised the gore-soaked stone a third time and let the blood coating it rain upon him. He pummeled Precious again and failed to flinch when the giant's blood spattered his face as the skull cracked and caved in, mashing its moist and spongy contents.

Ray's sanity crumbled. He screamed hysterically, slamming the rock down again. And again.

And again.

When Precious's body finally went still, Ray dropped the stone and limped away from the red, pulpy mass spread across the dirt.

He stumbled over to a tree and threw up. His hitched breathing turned into racking sobs and he collapsed onto his bloody knees. Cradling his pounding head, Ray wept for not only his dead brother, but for the loss of his own humanity. A line had been crossed. Things could not be unseen or undone.

And once again, his life changed in the blink of an eye where things would never be the same.

THIRTY-TWO

STANDING IN THE DINGY MOTEL bathroom with a towel around his waist, Ray wiped the condensation off the mirror and looked at his battered and bruised reflection under the strobing fluorescent lights. The scalding shower he'd just taken had turned the small room into a sauna, its steam already making him sweat.

His face was a puffy, purple mess. The cuts and scratches were now scabbed over but still glistening. His lip was split, his left eye nearly swollen shut. A molar worked loose by his tongue while showering sat on the bathtub drain, too large to be sucked down the metal grate.

He popped another painkiller then leaned in to assess the damage. Rachel's wedding band swung forward like a pendulum around his neck. He stared at it for a moment then looked back at the nearly unrecognizable face in the mirror.

After killing Precious, Ray forced himself to rise and made the long, torturous trek back to Jessie's farmhouse. With the purple sky threatening the approach of darkness, he couldn't afford to wander blindly in the woods at night, hoping to come across another house that most likely didn't exist. No, back at Jessie's, he had shelter, could tend to his wounds, and finally search the garage.

Once there, he cautiously entered the large barn doors, fearful another inbred might spring out for the kill like in the final, pre-credit jump scare of a bad horror movie. As the setting sun loomed over his shoulder, Ray grabbed a piece of rebar off the ground for protection ... just in case. Squinting in the gloom, he spotted Jessie's corpse at the far side of the garage. She lay on a filthy mattress with arms folded across her chest, her presentation one of peaceful grace. Before beginning his pursuit, Precious must have respectfully positioned his beloved as such and, inadvertently, granted Ray the much needed head start into the woods.

Ray hobbled over and searched her body. When his fingers felt the cold, jagged metal of the key's teeth in her front pocket, he whimpered and shook uncontrollably.

Gathering needed supplies—some food, water, a small first aid kit, and a shovel—Ray loaded the shrouded corpse of his brother into the bed of Jessie's pickup then used the jerry cans found out back to douse the house and garage in gasoline. He struck a match and let it all burn in order to erase their vile existence from the planet.

As the structures erupted into raging infernos, the red pickup disappeared into the cold darkness beyond the hellfire's glow. Then by the harsh beams of the truck's headlights, Eric was buried in a shallow grave well before the road turned paved and led back to the safety of the civilization dimly lit along the horizon. It was in this purgatory Ray said his goodbyes, both to his brother and to the part of himself taken that day.

Leaning forward on the bathroom sink, Ray continued his gaze into the motel mirror then looked at the wedding band hovering over his heart. He exhaled and lowered his head, knowing what needed to be done.

The motel room, resembling more of a mini-warehouse than an actual place of lodging, was stacked to its water-stained ceiling with boxes of stolen merchandise—tvs, laptops, cell phones, tablets, designer purses and shoes, cigarettes, liquor, and numerous other desirables.

Ray slowly finished dressing then limped between the cardboard aisles and took a seat on the rumpled bed. He struggled to slip on his shoes, wincing at the bruised ribs that painfully objected to his slightest movement. Pausing for a breather, he sat in silence and took in his surroundings.

The room, one among many, was where "Fatty" McPhattins kept his booty. The rundown hotel just outside the Fort Worth Stockyards was used as a warehouse for stolen goods. Select rooms in front were made available for lodging in order to keep up appearances, but guests were far and few between because of the decrepit condition of the place. Rooms at the back of the establishment— hidden from prying eyes—were used for loading and unloading hot merchandise, as well as a place for Ray to clean up and rest for a few hours before continuing on his mission.

He'd called ahead before arriving at the motel, letting Fatty know he was on his way. And he would be alone. He gave him a list of needed supplies and a heads up that his stolen vehicle would need disposing of.

And now, after a few hours of rest, a hot shower, re-dressing his wounds, and a change of clothes provided by Fatty, Ray sat on the bed and glanced over at the half-empty bottle of Jack Daniel's on the nightstand and the tattered, bloodstained envelope sitting next to it.

Ray stared at the envelope and fidgeted with the wedding band on his finger.

The morbidly obese man sitting behind the motel counter definitely lived up to his nickname. Mark "Fatty" McPhattins had a cell phone glued to his ear in one hand and an open two-liter diet soda in the other. While listening to the caller, he raised the plastic bottle and took a series of gulps then nodded and blew out a burp as stealthily as possible.

"Got it," Fatty said. He glanced up and saw Ray approaching the office. The man was limping and carrying a large, bulky duffel bag stuffed tight.

The tinkle of a bell over the door announced Ray's entrance. Fatty locked eyes with him and nodded.

"Uh-huh," he grunted into the cell.

Ray turned to the window overlooking the front parking lot. A black Ford Explorer with tinted windows was aimed in their direction.

"Yep," Fatty continued. "All right. I'll let him know." He clicked off the cell and laid it on top of the newspaper he'd been reading before receiving the call.

Ray pointed his chin at the Explorer. "That mine?"

Fatty reached under the counter for the keys then tossed them at him. "As requested." He eyed the duffle bag. "And I see you found the other stuff I left out for ya."

Ray gave the bag a shake and nodded. "Thanks, man. I owe ya."

"You don't owe me shit. You guys are like family."

They exchanged a look. Fatty had been told about Eric before Ray's arrival. Which gave Fatty plenty of time to go out behind the office and stomp the metal trashcans flat. When finished, the rage he felt quickly turned to blubbering as he lamented the loss of a dear friend.

Fatty cleared his throat so his voice wouldn't crack. "Somethin' else you should know." He nodded to the cell on the counter. "Just got word that LaMorte's dispatched multiple crews. To get back what's his."

Ray stood silent.

"And you know how it works with him, man." Fatty continued. "Even with Eric ..." he exhaled and shrugged meekly, "gone... his debt rolls over onto you."

Ray sighed. "Yeah. We'll just have to see how that works out, now won't we?"

Fatty glanced back down at the duffle bag in Ray's hand and cracked a smile, showcasing the large gap between his front teeth. "Yep. Guess so."

"One more thing," Ray said.

"Anything."

"Put your ear to the ground and find out who hired this guy I'm about to visit. I want to confirm what I pull out of him. Start with the owners of the last job we did three years back. Montego Silver Exchange in Round Rock. They must have been connected. Find out to who. Which family."

"Will do."

Slowly inhaling, Ray nodded at Fatty, a gesture equaling both goodbye and thank you. Then he turned and limped out of the office.

Fatty watched him climb into the Explorer and drive out of the parking lot.

He stared out the window and his heart sunk over the fact it was probably the last time he'd ever see Ray again. What the man was chasing was equally as dangerous as what was now pursuing him. The odds were definitely not in his favor.

"Godspeed, brother," Fatty whispered, then forced himself to look away.

As the sun peeked over the horizon, Ray sat behind the wheel of the Explorer, guiding it down the long stretch of Interstate 35. He slid on dark sunglasses that concealed his swollen, black eye and rolled down the window for some fresh air.

After checking his rearview, he scratched his stubbled cheek and focused on the road ahead. He did a double take at the upcoming sign and cracked a bittersweet smile. Ray opened the center console and pulled out the bloodstained envelope.

Removing the directions, he held the paper up for a quick review and cast aside its stained casing.

A gust of wind caught the envelope, whipping it up and over the backseat and into the Explorer's cargo area. The paper fluttered and landed on top of the large duffle bag, partially unzipped, revealing the arsenal inside—the sawed-off shotgun, various pistols, boxes of ammunition, rope, duct tape, needle nose pliers, ball peen hammer, gardening shears and various other instruments of torture.

Ray folded up the directions and stuck the paper under his leg to keep it safe and within reach. He white-knuckled the steering wheel with his left hand. His wedding band was gone, replaced by the untanned strip of skin the ring had protected for over a dozen years.

As the Explorer shot down the highway, it roared past the large green sign that simply read ...

WELCOME TO OKLAHOMA.

Acknowlegements

Thanks to Scott Kurtz and Jason Croft for helping me map this road trip from hell many, many years ago. It's been a long journey and has gone through various incarnations but it's finally leaving home for the world to see. Thanks to C.V. Hunt and Andersen Prunty for their hard work in making it look so much better. And thank you to Kristopher Triana for suggesting I send this novel to the fine folks at Grindhouse Press when I was trying to find it a good home.

ABOUT THE AUTHOR

A former filmmaker and screenwriter, Matt Kurtz wisely transitioned to novels and short stories and now doesn't have to worry about going over budget or over schedule when writing his tales. He's had over fifty short stories published, some of which now comprise his collections *Monkey's Box of Horrors - Tales of Terror: Volume 1* and *Monkey's Bucket of Horrors - Tales of Terror: Volume 2*. Matt recently completed his second novel, a horror story about witches. He lives somewhere in the state of Texas with an extreme phobia of spiders and naked old women (don't ask ... seriously).

Other Grindhouse Press Titles